She was carrying his child.

He felt shaken to his very foundations. Nothing in life had braced him for this eventuality.

And yet now, as he stared down at her, what should have horrified him, didn't. What should have filled him with resentment, didn't. He didn't feel the walls closing in. Instead, he felt a surge of protectiveness that rocked him.

Where did *that* come from?

He'd never factored children into his life. Why would he? He'd seen the damage parents could do, lived the unspoken sorrow born of growing up with the whiff of abandonment.

So having kids? Never been on the horizon. Easier to shelve that whole issue than take the risk of being an unwitting cause of hurt to a kid who hadn't asked to be born. He worked all the hours under the sun. That, for starters, augured badly for the sort of family lifestyle children needed.

And yet...

Leandro had an insane desire to take this woman away, wrap her up in cotton wool and protect her because she was now the mother of his unborn child.

Cathy Williams can remember reading Harlequin books as a teenager, and now that she is writing them, she remains an avid fan. For her, there is nothing like creating romantic stories and engaging plots, and each and every book is a new adventure. Cathy lives in London, and her three daughters—Charlotte, Olivia and Emma—have always been, and continue to be, the greatest inspirations in her life.

Books by Cathy Williams

Harlequin Presents

The Forbidden Cabrera Brother
Desert King's Surprise Love-Child
Consequences of Their Wedding Charade
Hired by the Forbidden Italian

Secrets of the Stowe Family

Forbidden Hawaiian Nights
Promoted to the Italian's Fiancée
Claiming His Cinderella Secretary

Visit the Author Profile page
at Harlequin.com for more titles.

Cathy Williams

—

BOUND BY A NINE-MONTH CONFESSION

◆ HARLEQUIN
PRESENTS

**HARLEQUIN®
PRESENTS™**

Recycling programs
for this product may
not exist in your area.

ISBN-13: 978-1-335-58365-9

Bound by a Nine-Month Confession

Copyright © 2022 by Cathy Williams

For questions and comments about the quality of this book,
please contact us at CustomerService@Harlequin.com.

Harlequin Enterprises ULC
22 Adelaide St. West, 41st Floor
Toronto, Ontario M5H 4E3, Canada
www.Harlequin.com

Printed in U.S.A.

BOUND BY A NINE-MONTH CONFESSION

To Hannah, for being a lovely and encouraging editor.

CHAPTER ONE

'*WHAT?*'

It had taken a few seconds for Celia to register what her client was saying.

'What do you mean, you've decided not to get married after all...?'

She levered herself up from where she had been kneeling, meticulously pinning the hem of the dress she was making.

A wedding dress.

Not in the traditional white because this was marriage number two for Julie Raymond. This was a pale lilac creation, exquisitely beautiful and threaded with hundreds of tiny pearls, each of which had been laboriously sewn on by hand.

Three months of toing and froing over the design, four months of time-consuming putting together with dozens of fittings, at each of which something had had to be changed. Then there was the time spent sourcing just the right fabric from just the right factory with just the right eco-friendly credentials.

Not so much a labour of love as a roller-coaster ride underlaid with simmering panic that the creation in the making might not come to fruition in time for the big day because of the number of roadblocks that kept appearing on the journey.

But here they were, with the wedding a week away and…

Celia stared up at her client in consternation, her green eyes urgently questioning. The expression on Julie's face was enough to slam shut the door on any notions that she might have misheard. The wedding of the year was being called off.

Should warning bells have started clanging months ago? Should she have paid more attention to throwaway remarks that had become more persistent over the past few weeks?

It wasn't as if Julie hadn't confided in her, snippets about her past and the loveless marriage she had endured for four years. She had wed an earl only to discover that with the title came the expectation that he be allowed to continue his womanising bachelor ways, untroubled by the humdrum monotony of married life. The divorce had been protracted and exhausting, Julie had confided bitterly.

So yes, Celia had had insights into her client and slowly they had formed an easy camaraderie, a closeness that sometimes happened between people whose lives ran on different railway tracks. It was the closeness between one with a need to confide and another with an ability to listen, two people who didn't share the same social platform. It was a safe place for Julie because confidences shared never risked being leaked to mutual friends.

'I can't go through with it.'

Celia rested back on her haunches and waited until Julie had stepped down from the squat box on which she had been standing. Then she ushered her upstairs into the tiny kitchen, away from the main body of the shop with its fitting rooms and racks of clothes in the process of being made and the busyness of her two assistants with their clients.

Julie Raymond was an absolutely stunning and statuesque blonde. A dream of a model who could have worn a bin bag and still looked spectacular.

She towered over Celia, who was secretly in awe of her, from her well-behaved, sleek, shiny bob to the impeccably manicured perfection of her fingernails.

The long-sleeved wedding dress, lovingly hugging a willowy body, trailed half pinned and in miserable disarray along the ground, picking up dust along the way.

'You're just a little nervous,' Celia soothed, seamlessly segueing into agony aunt mode. 'The wedding is only a few days away and life as you know it is going to change but, Julie...you mustn't let your past ruin a wonderful future. I know you had a...um...*disappointing* first marriage, but that was years ago and I'm sure that...er... Leandro will be a wonderful husband...'

'Maybe.' Julie laughed with carefree abandon and rested the mug of tea that had been handed to her on her lap. 'But definitely not to me.'

What could Celia say to that? How could she wax lyrical about the virtues of someone she had never met?

Not once had the adoring husband-to-be arranged to collect his fiancée so that he could whisk her off to a romantic meal after one of her very many late evening fittings.

Nor, come to think of it, had Julie mentioned him very much at all and, when quizzed, had been conspicuously mealy-mouthed on the subject of the love of her life.

She had vaguely hinted that she had known him for absolutely ages and if she had failed to follow this up with the usual glowing reports of how wonderful he was, then, camaraderie or no camaraderie, that was not Celia's business. At the end of the day, she was being paid to do a job and an important one. A huge job for an extravagant wedding where her dress would be the star of the show and, for three young girls climbing the career ladder in the competitive world of fashion design, a real opportunity.

'You wouldn't understand,' Julie said gently, and Celia frowned.

She could see the faintest of tea-ring stains from the mug on the pale lilac.

'Of course I do,' she said. 'You have cold feet. It happens. One minute you're looking forward to a shiny bright future and the next minute you're terrified that you'll be giving up all the freedoms that come with singledom...'

'And have you ever been there, Celia? Torn between the shiny bright future and the allure of singledom?'

Celia flushed and, for a few seconds, she felt the breath leave her body.

Had she ever been there? On the brink of marriage with all its glorious possibilities and dreams and hopes?

Yes! Once upon a time when she'd been just nineteen, engaged to the boy literally only a few doors away, the boy she had known for ever. He'd been her best friend, her confidant and then, when they'd both turned sixteen, her boyfriend. In the little village where they'd both grown up, deep in the heart of the countryside, they'd simply drifted into sealing a union that had been expected of them by both sets of parents.

Celia knew now that the best thing Martin had ever done had been to break things off but still…it had hurt. She'd smiled at the time, and held her head high until her jaw had ached. She'd assured her parents that it had been a joint decision, that they were both way too young anyway, that they'd rushed into things…and wasn't it a blessing that they'd seen sense before it was too late?

But she could still remember the tightness in her chest and the sadness that the wedding dress she'd been making, a labour of love because she'd just nailed her sewing course and had been excited to try out her newly qualified skills, would never be used.

It was neatly folded in a bag in a cupboard, a permanent reminder that when it came to giving her heart away, she would only do so with a clear head. A reminder that what you thought was love was all too often disguised as something else and if you got taken in, you ended up with an unused wedding dress gathering cobwebs in a cupboard. For her, the thrill of being engaged and planning for a wedding had papered over the blunt reality, which was that she and Martin had never been *in love*. They'd been a couple of kids who had allowed the tide to drift them this way and that.

Martin had found someone else in record time, someone athletic and into all the outdoor pursuits he had loved and which Celia had stoically endured. He had found his soulmate, had even asked Celia to attend his wedding, which she had politely declined. He had moved on. But for her? It didn't matter how much she told herself that she was in a better place single than she would have been in a marriage that would have ended in bitterness and acrimony. The scales would have fallen from both their eyes and reality would have eventually intruded on their youthful, impossible bubble and they wouldn't have remained friends, that was for sure! And what if a child had been involved? How tangled would *that* have been?

But Celia knew that the experience had taken that carefree side of her and curdled it. She was so careful now, so cautious…and

Julie's throwaway question seemed to have brought it all to the surface. Briefly.

'We're not talking about me, Julie.' She smiled stiffly, eager to swivel the focus away from her. 'So don't try to change the subject.'

Actually, now that she happened to glance at Julie's finger, the engagement ring appeared to have been well and truly ditched. When had that happened and how had she failed to notice?

Celia felt an uncharitable spurt of irritation and banked it down.

Yes, Julie's first marriage had been a disaster. But she had moved on to find someone else, someone she presumably loved enough to accept his marriage proposal, and here she was now, washing her hands of it all in a couple of airily nonchalant sentences. Not a remorseful tear in sight.

'I've worked with many brides-to-be, Julie, and there's always some nerves beforehand.'

'I haven't actually been nervous about getting married.'

'What does Leandro have to say?' Celia swerved away from all non-starter chat about her client's lack of pre-wedding nerves, her refusal to consider the most likely reason for her calling off the marriage at the eleventh hour. 'He must be…heartbroken.'

Did she care about the now fast-vanishing prospect of her stunning wedding gown getting the coverage she had so hoped for? Maybe propelling them into the big league?

Yes, she did.

But more than that, Celia came from a traditional family. She and her brother both did. Their parents had married young and were still in love decades later. A straightforward life with a straightforward outcome. When she thought of the grief and unhappiness opening up at Julie's feet, at Leandro's feet, she felt a wrench of sadness for them both.

How was it that Julie seemed so blithely unaware of the ramifications of her snap decision?

Couldn't she see what she was casually tossing aside? Didn't she know how very lucky she was to be with a guy who loved her? That you didn't get love just to throw it away on an anxious whim? Because you figured that something better might be just around the corner? Didn't she realise that there were women out there with unused wedding dresses stuck in the back of cupboards, melancholy testament to dreams that had never come true?

'If you met Leandro,' Julie said thoughtfully, 'I'm not sure *heartbroken* would ever be a word you could use to describe how he might feel in a situation like this.'

'But I've never met him.'

'He's a very busy man.'

Celia frowned, tempted to pry further but conscious that she had no role to play in Julie's decision. She wasn't a counsellor, and it wasn't her job to try and talk anyone out of anything!

But what a shame and what a waste.

She'd worked with wedding dresses for years. She'd ironically thought how odd it was that from her own abandoned wedding dress, lovingly sewn in anticipation of the big day that never came, had come an absolute love for the intricacies of making wedding dresses.

The attention to detail…the little personal requests some brides-to-be asked to be sewn into bodice tops, under lace…once in the lining…

She had never once felt in the slightest bit envious that all these dresses, made by her and her team, would usher in lives filled with hope and happiness while for her…who knew when her own day would come?

But as she listened to Julie kindly telling her how much she loved the dress, plucking at the expensive fabric and frowning with an expression of mild dismay at the faint mark left by the mug she had rested on it, Celia couldn't help but feel a wave of self-pity. She had chosen to tread carefully, which meant that she was on her own now as much as she had been when she and Martin had broken up. Being on her own seemed to have become a career choice. And here was Julie, wedding dress already stained and soon to be ditched, tossing aside her chance at happiness with a shrug.

'You'll be paid for it, of course,' her client was expanding now. 'You've done an amazing job and I'm going to recommend you to all my friends. You'll have so much lovely business, Celia, you'll be rushed off your feet!'

Celia smiled weakly and gave up on trying to play agony aunt.

She felt drained. Memories had jumped out at her just when she didn't need them and now she wanted to close the shop and head back to the small house she rented in Shepherd's Bush.

'I'm really sorry, Julie,' she said gently, removing the mug, taking it to the sink and then remaining there, standing, waiting for her client to do likewise, which she didn't, until Celia prompted, 'It's nearly time for me to be closing up for the evening.'

'I should mention that I've met someone,' Julie blurted out with sudden nervousness.

'You've *met someone*?'

'Um…'

'But when? How? I had no idea! Not, of course, that it's any of my business, although maybe you should have thought about breaking things off with Leandro earlier? Look, Julie, I really need to close the shop now. We can sort all the details about the dress later. There's no need for you to tell me the ins and outs of your private life. It's very sad that you won't be marrying Leandro but it's your life and, of course, I wish you well.'

She purposefully wiped the kitchen counter and headed to the door, her body language signalling the end of the conversation. She could feel a headache coming on.

'It's the real thing, Celia. I can tell from your expression that you disapprove but, honestly, this guy…? He's the real deal.'

'I… I'm happy for you, Julie, I really am, but—'

'And there's something else I think you should know…'

'Really?' Celia raised her eyebrows. She wondered what more could possibly be on the agenda. A final fitting had turned into the confession to end all confessions and her brain hurt when she thought about not just Julie's poor fiancé but the sheer nightmare of unpicking what had been touted as the wedding of the year. Where did you even start on that?

'The guy I'm seeing? It happens to be your brother...'

Celia was still reeling from that shock announcement two days later as she began putting away stuff in the workshop, ready to lock up and head to the Underground.

Knocked for six and frantically thinking that she surely must have misheard, she had listened with mounting horror as Julie had given her a brief synopsis of her life-changing fling with Dan.

From standing in a purposeful manner, she had collapsed like a rag doll right back into the chair from which she had earlier risen.

How on earth had her brother crept into this scenario?

She had found out fast enough.

Yes, they had met. Quite by chance, as it happened. A couple of months ago, Julie had turned up for a fitting and Dan had been there, in all his good-looking glory. He had rocked up on his motorbike to hand-deliver a book he had promised Celia.

Celia remembered the day quite clearly because she had done her best to hustle him out. She adored her older brother but life, for him, moved on his own timeline and she had been rushed off her feet with a list of things to get through before she left.

Had he and Julie chatted? Sure. Celia had barely noticed. Julie was a besotted bride-to-be. Why would Celia have paid a scrap of attention to the fact that her brother had hung around for longer than he should have, chatting?

Dan was a chatty person! Five years older, he was completely different from her...from looks to personality.

Tall to her short...dark-haired to her red... and carefree in ways she had always envied and admired.

Had Julie fallen for that?

She'd said that Leandro was something of a workaholic. Had Dan's breezy insouciance delivered a mortal hammer blow to a bride whose head had been filled with sudden, last-minute doubts about the guy she was marrying? Had the guy who had gone freelance because he spurned the tyranny of a nine-to-five work schedule charmed the woman destined to wed a man chained to a desk?

Had opposites attracted in what had been a perfect but temporary storm?

At any rate, she had been swamped with guilt. If Dan had never been there, Julie would still be going ahead with her marriage and whatever nerves she was experiencing would have fizzled out like dew in the summer sun.

Instead...

Celia had tried to get hold of her brother, but he had gone underground and when she'd carefully tried to find out whether her parents were any the wiser, she had quickly realised that they weren't. 'You know your brother,' Lizzie Drew had said with maternal indulgence. 'Never one for the details of where he is!'

Celia was beginning to wonder whether she knew her brother at all.

Absorbed in the same train of thought that had been cluttering her head for the past two days, she was only aware of the doorbell ringing downstairs after it had gone from staccato bursts to one long, insistent, demanding and intensely annoying buzz.

She hurried down the short flight of stairs into the display area of her shop, banging on the lights at the bottom.

It was cold and dark outside, and the January air was heavy with the promise of snow, predicted but thus far yet to fall.

A miserable time of thick cardigans and coats and waterproofs and the dreary daily trudge, fighting the elements and the crowds to get to the Tube.

The Closed sign was on the door, clearly visible to anyone with twenty-twenty vision.

She pulled open the door, mouth half open to state the obvious, hand raised to indicate the sign on the door, and then it fell back.

Startled eyes travelled up and up and up to a face that was so absolutely perfect in its olive-toned symmetry that her mouth fell open and for a few seconds her head went completely blank.

Leandro stared back at the redhead in front of him in silence.

So this was the woman whose name had been mentioned with increasing regularity for the past year. Not quite what he had been expecting although, to be fair, he hadn't had any clear image of anyone in his head.

'Can I help you?' She pointed to the sign that he had seen and ignored. 'I was just about to head off...perhaps whatever you want could wait until tomorrow morning? I'm here most days by eight.'

He detected a thread of annoyance in her voice and conceded that she had every reason to be annoyed but needs must. He didn't want to be here any more than she wanted him here. 'I'd rather not,' he drawled.

'You'd *rather not*?'

'I'd rather not.' He tempered his bluntness with something of a smile, although it was damned difficult because this was no smiling situation. Not by a long shot. He raked his fingers through his hair, glanced away with a frown and then added, carefully, eyes pinned to her face, 'Believe me, I don't make a habit of showing up unannounced anywhere...but I assure you, this is important and it's urgent I talk to you.'

He watched carefully as she digested what he'd said. She had a remarkably transparent face. A useful asset in a wedding-dress designer, he imagined, programmed as he was from a young age to be cynical. A bride-to-be would want an emotional and empathetic listening ear at an emotional and exciting time. All those happy-ever-after endings in sight... all those fairy tales about to turn a corner and come true...what better than someone pinning and sewing with an encouraging smile and appealing, puppy-dog eyes?

Appealing puppy-dog eyes the colour of green glass washed up on a beach?

Everything about the woman oozed just the sort of softness that would encourage a bride to open up and share her secrets.

Leandro, who had received a three-sentence message from Julie two days previously, was in no doubt that, whatever was going on, the small redhead in front of him would have the explanation and he wasn't leaving until he got it.

Where the heck was his fiancée?

He'd thought he and Julie had a pretty good understanding of the situation. No blurred lines or room for error. But he'd been wrong.

I'm so sorry but I can't go through with the wedding, Leandro. It's not you. It's me.

What the hell did *that* mean?

Nor had she graced her father with anything more illuminating and that in itself had infuriated Leandro, because the old guy deserved better.

Were there dots waiting to be joined? Had he missed the link somehow? He never missed links and he was excellent when it came to joining dots so what was going on here?

'You're interested in commissioning a dress... Mr...?'

'I'm interested in the whereabouts of someone who's recently commissioned a dress from you, Miss Drew,' he said quietly.

'Who *are* you?' Celia's heart was thudding. She wasn't used to the impact of a guy on her like this and she didn't like it. It made her feel exposed, because she had spent so long distancing herself from involvement with the opposite sex, happy to bide her time until the right guy came along. She'd been hurt once and she could still remember how that had felt, could remember it enough to know that if she held back, if no one could really get to her, then she would never be hurt again.

She hadn't budged from where she was standing, blocking entry to the shop.

The man, whoever he was, commanded her full attention, pinning her to the spot. An aura of dark danger emanated from him.

She wasn't used to this sort of powerful, self-assured and masculine presence.

'Let me in, Miss Drew. Please.'

'Sorry, but no.'

'I really need to talk to you and it's a conversation that can't be conducted on a pavement.'

'In that case, you can always make an appointment like everyone else. Like I said, I'm here from eight most mornings.'

'I need to talk to you about Julie. My name is Leandro. I'm her fiancé. Or…' he smiled wryly '…should I say *ex*-fiancé? I seem to be caught in an evolving situation.'

She was staring at him, lips pursed, arms folded, welcome mat fully retracted.

In every respect, she was as far removed from the women he was accustomed to as chalk was from cheese. Her clothes were comfy, shapeless. A pair of loose trousers, an extremely baggy shirt, an even baggier cardigan and a tape measure around her neck, which he assumed she had forgotten about in her haste to get the door.

Everything seemed to be in various shades of grey and black, but she was rescued from inevitable plainness by the amazing vibrancy of her copper-coloured hair, the way it rioted around her heart-shaped face in rebellious disarray, and crystal-clear green eyes that were framed by sooty dark gold lashes. And, of course, freckles. A lot of them.

'*You're* Leandro…'

'Will you let me in, Miss Drew? It *is* Miss, isn't it? Julie never clarified so feel free to correct me if I've jumped to conclusions?'

'Yes, I'm *Ms* Drew, Celia, and okay, I guess you'd better come in.'

'I appreciate that,' he told her. 'It's dark. You're in the process of locking up to go home. You don't know who the heck might be knocking on your door, so thank you for trusting me. Like I said, I wouldn't have descended on your doorstep if it wasn't important.'

Her breath hitched as he swept past her, bringing in the cold air with him.

Under the glare of the overhead lights, she now had an up-close-and-personal view of just how spectacular the guy was.

He towered over her, at least six-three to her five-four, and his hair was raven black and cut short, which emphasised the harsh contours of his face with its sensual mouth, straight nose and slashing cheekbones.

'You'd better come upstairs.' He still made her heart skitter inside her and her nerves were all over the place but something about him, something about the sincerity of his words, made her realise that the guy was to be trusted.

And what did she imagine he was going to do anyway? She was as safe as houses around a guy like him! Just one glance at his elegant, beautiful fiancée and any fool would be able to work out that he was a man who liked tall and elegant. Not petite and far too sensible.

She spun round on her heel and headed up, acutely conscious of him behind her, as stealthy as a jungle cat.

This was not what she'd been expecting.

When she'd eventually shown Julie the door two days previously, she had been too shell-shocked to ask detailed questions about what plans she and Dan had made. The Dan connection had been enough to blow all those obvious questions out of the water. She had just gaped in silence like a stranded goldfish as Julie, liberated from having to keep everything under wraps, had opened up with enthusiasm about the thrilling journey of her wonderful affair.

Celia had assumed that her brother was diplomatically ducking the worst of the fallout for as long as he could. She'd, however, taken it as a given that Julie would have been more forthcoming with the guy she'd jilted, yet here he was now, seeking answers to questions.

Of course, he would know about her own personal connection to the messy, sorry saga. Did he intend to lay the blame at her door? Somehow? None of it was her fault but she knew that, in times of extreme stress, it was normal to divert all blame onto the shoulders of someone else. The alternative would be for him to look inwards and try and question his own role in what had happened and, judging from what she'd seen so far, this guy didn't seem to be the sort who spent too much time soul-searching.

'I have tea or coffee,' she said, reluctantly turning to face him and struck once again by the sheer beauty of his perfectly arranged features. He dwarfed the tiny kitchen and seemed to suck the oxygen out of the air so that she felt breathless and addled.

'Coffee. Black. Shall we do away with the chit-chat? What exactly did Julie say to you?'

'Say?'

Leandro raised his eyebrows in wry questioning, utterly relaxed in the chair he had taken. 'The one name that's crossed my ex-fiancée's lips for the past few months has been yours. It seems that she's built up some kind of bond with you, which in turn leads me to conclude that you know where she is, and I would very much like to find that out.'

No beating about the bush. Celia could feel the prized self-control she had learned to exercise begin to slip away, buffeted by the sheer force of his personality.

Did he think he could breeze in here and prise information out of her? Information his fiancée, for reasons Celia might not be able to fathom or condone, had seen fit to with-hold from him?

She fiddled with her hair, twirled the ends between her fingers. 'Why would I tell you if I knew where she was?' she eventually asked. 'If Julie hasn't told you where she's going, then perhaps it's because she doesn't want you to know, and if she doesn't want you to know, then it's not up to me to go against her wishes.'

But how could she understand the ques-tions he must want to ask, questions only Julie could answer, which was why he had shown up here on her doorstep? Hadn't she spent days and weeks analysing her own break-up? Even though she and Martin had talked about it, even though she'd known why it had ended? It was basic human nature. Le-andro had been about to walk up the aisle only to find that the woman he was in love with had decided to do a runner with another man. It was heartbreaking, really.

He wanted answers and, because Julie had failed to provide them, he had come to Celia seeking some sort of balm for his aching soul.

Granted, as they stared at one another, his dark, saturnine face coolly remote and watchful, as she felt a shiver of something steal through her body like quicksilver, she couldn't help but think that he didn't look at all like a guy with an aching soul.

Still...

She sighed, prepared to give him the benefit of the doubt.

'I actually don't have the answers to your questions,' she confessed. 'I wish I had, but no. I have no idea where Julie and my brother have gone. Not a clue.'

Leandro stilled, sat forward and looked at her with laser-sharp concentration.

'Your brother? What does *your brother* have to do with this...?'

CHAPTER TWO

LEANDRO WATCHED THE slow burn of colour invade her cheeks. She might have thought that he was in the dark about Julie's whereabouts, but it was obvious that, whatever she'd been thinking, it hadn't occurred to her that his ex-fiancée might have vanished withholding the most important piece of information in the whole, sorry scenario.

Another man.

Not even on the very edges of his consciousness had another man featured in Julie's disappearance. When it came to the opposite sex, she had had her fill of men, or so she had assured him on countless occasions. Wasn't that why their arranged marriage had seemed such a good idea at the time? No unrealistic dreams to be shattered. Just cool, practical reasoning to create a solution for a problem that had arisen out of the blue with her father, like the sudden onset of a storm rolling in from distant horizons, bringing with it the promise of catastrophe.

And for him? What would he be sacrificing by a marriage of convenience? Dreams of everlasting love with a good woman? Starry-eyed, romantic notions of fairy-tale happiness? No. Far from it.

Leandro had learned from a young age that love was a weakness to be avoided at all costs. Lust and hot sex? Yes. Those were things he could control, but love? No. Love was pain and loss and vulnerability, and he had seen from a young age what that side of the happy-ever-after coin was all about.

He didn't remember his mother, because she had walked out when he'd been a toddler. One minute there, the next minute not. She'd dumped his dad for the glitter of jangling gold coins in a rich man's pocket. He knew that she'd been a beautiful woman, because his father had hung onto all the pictures that he'd taken of her that used to sit on tables and shelves until, at the age of eight, Leandro had methodically gathered them all up and dumped them in the bin. Had his father rescued them? He would never know because they'd never again reappeared on the tables and shelves. Perhaps he'd known that if he'd ever brought them out again, Leandro would have done the same thing all over again, because what child needed to be reminded that he'd been abandoned by his own mother?

His father had never managed to patch up what had been left of his broken heart. In later years, he had told Leandro about the dreams he and Isabella Diaz had had and that, in the end, he just hadn't been rich enough for her. He'd been clever and handsome, but a clever and handsome workman on a ranch hadn't stood a chance against a rich, young guy who had come to visit and had ended up leaving with his pretty young wife.

By the time Leandro was old enough to understand the ways of the world, he had learnt a valuable lesson. His father had shown him the things he wanted to get out of life—financial security and complete control of his destiny—and the way to get those was to avoid the pitfalls of handing your heart over to anyone.

He and Julie had had an understanding and he'd liked the arrangement they'd had.

But now, a man had entered the equation and he intended to find out just how that had come about.

There wasn't a shred of gullibility in him and, for the first time, he looked around, really taking in his surroundings.

What did he see here? A talented seam-stress working hard to make a decent living. One who had suddenly found herself work-ing on a wedding dress for a confiding cli-ent with a lineage as long as your arm and a family pile in Northumberland.

Was it coincidence that her brother had ap-peared from nowhere?

That Julie, in the space of a few days...or weeks...was suddenly smitten enough to dis-appear with a guy she barely knew?

Was money at the root of it all?

Suspicion was so much a part and parcel of Leandro's DNA that that was the very first route he felt he needed to explore, because he was having a hard time marrying the image of his lovely but ice-cool fiancée caught in the throes of illicit passion with a virtual stranger. It made it all the more impossible to believe that this improbable whirlwind fling was any-thing other than a clever conman working on a vulnerable woman.

'So...' He sat forward now and pushed the mug of coffee to the side with one finger so that he could rest his arms on the table, narrowing the space between them. 'I'm in-trigued. Where does your brother fit into all of this?'

'What did Julie tell you?'

'I've never been much of a fan of anyone who answers a question with a question,' he murmured drily, his dark eyes watchful and speculative. 'And I don't want to waste time playing games. I'm guessing that Julie and your brother have embarked on some kind of affair?'

'I'm sorry.'

Leandro waved that aside, his mind galloping towards an explanation. 'When? When did it all start?'

'I honestly don't know.'

'Sure about that?'

'What do you mean?'

'Tell me about your brother.' Leandro abruptly pulled back from voicing his suspicions. He wanted a clearer picture, and it was beginning to seem that the brief question-and-answer session he had had in mind wasn't going to go down the predicted route.

But attack wasn't usually the best way to elicit information. Everyone deserved a fair hearing even though, in true Hansel and Gretel style, the trail of crumbs seemed to be heading in a very predictable direction, directly to the gingerbread house.

He tilted his head to one side and watched as she softened, and half smiled. An indulgent, loving sister who seemed to be in awe and admiration of an older brother who, from the sounds of it, was the sort of free spirit Leandro, personally, really didn't get.

Momentarily distracted, he halted her in mid flow and said, with genuine curiosity, 'You admire the fact that he doesn't own anything even though he's...what? Pushing thirty?'

Celia smiled. 'He's a free spirit.'

'And what's there to admire about that?' The *free spirit*, it appeared, used a motorbike as his primary mode of transport and lived, by choice, in rented accommodation because the harsh realities of getting a mortgage represented just too much of a headache for someone who refused to be ruled by all the normal things that most people set their compass by.

'Haven't you ever wanted to be free of...a nine-to-five job?'

'I don't actually have a nine-to-five job.'

'No,' Celia mused thoughtfully. 'You're a workaholic.'

'Is that what Julie told you?'

Celia flushed. 'She wasn't being critical,' she inserted quickly. 'She was just being honest.'

'But moving back to the subject of your brother...' He absently wondered what it was about the woman that threw him. Was it because there was something refreshing about her? Something that made him think that she was being utterly honest in her responses even though so much of him was primed never to take what anyone said at face value, especially in circumstances such as this?

If her brother had made a play for Julie because of the family fortune he believed she had, then was his sister complicit in any way?

For once, he hesitated to pursue cold, hard suspicions. That said, he'd never shied away from anything in his life before and he wasn't about to start now.

His dark eyes didn't leave her face.

'What I'm thinking is that all of this has happened very, very suddenly. Along comes your fun-loving brother with his disdain for all things material, and in a matter of seconds he's swept my aristocratic fiancée off her feet and whisked her away to who knows where. Is it just me or does that feel a little… suspicious? Maybe I'm being over-cynical, but there's a lot of truth in the saying that money makes the world go round…even to a fun-loving free spirit who doesn't care about the cost of a loaf of bread…'

His accusations filled the space between them, and Leandro watched as she paled, absorbing what he was saying and probably reading between the lines to what he wasn't.

'How dare you?'

'I had no idea Julie was involved with someone else.'

'My brother would never...*never*...get involved with someone for the wrong reasons!'

'You're very trusting when it comes to human nature. From experience, I've found it wiser to steer clear of blindly believing what I'm told.' He sat forward, his expression suddenly urgent. 'It's important that I find Julie, Miss Drew.'

'Celia...' Her voice was distracted, her expression tense; she was dismayed by the accusations that were rolling around in her head.

But wasn't there a part of her that could understand, not only why he had shown up here, but why he had jumped to the conclusions that he had?

He'd accused her of being trusting, but wasn't she just the opposite? She'd been burnt once and no amount of cool-headed reasoning about the narrow escape she'd had had been able to stop her from building walls around herself when it came to men.

The last thing she was was *trusting* and yet she knew that, underneath her own heartbreak, she still believed in love. It would never have occurred to her that something as tawdry as money could ever influence someone's behaviour, and certainly not Dan's. But the wealthy were often objects of pursuit, so why wouldn't he immediately jump to the conclusion that a guy who was a self-confessed free spirit might find the temptation of a rich and beautiful woman irresistible? He was wrong about her brother…but that didn't mean he might not have grounds for suspicion, did it? Especially if he was suspicious by nature.

She wondered what those experiences were that had made this man so cynical. People were shaped by what life threw at them, and as their eyes met and tangled she felt a sharp stab of curiosity that was momentarily powerful enough to sweep away the raw anger at his accusations.

There was no place for curiosity, though. This was a straightforward situation, insofar as she had no idea where Julie and her brother had gone. When she glanced at her watch, it was to find that more time had gone by than she'd expected.

'I'm very sorry about what's happened… Mr…'

'Leandro.'

'Yes, well, I'm sorry that Julie has run off

with my brother. I did try to talk her out of it, tried to tell her that it was just a case of pre-wedding nerves. But she'd made her mind up. I know that's probably not what you want to hear, but...' She hesitated but then figured that if he felt free to say exactly what was on his mind, whether it was offensive or not, then why shouldn't she? 'People fall in love and it might just be the case that Julie and Dan have fallen in love, in which case what's the point in trying to find them? What will you hope to gain? And if you're still keen to track them down...' she shrugged, hardly believing that the cool, controlled man staring at her with such brooding intensity could be capable of the sort of wild passion that would propel him to hunt down a woman who had jilted him '...then surely you can just hire someone?'

Leandro looked at her in silence for a few seconds, then he stood up and moved towards the door.

'It would seem that that's the last remaining option,' he murmured and then he smiled and, just for a moment, Celia felt the breath whoosh out of her because she had a glimpse of the sort of devastating charm that could knock a person off her feet. 'And just for the record...' his voice was dry and amused '...

this isn't about love. This is much bigger and more important than that. My apologies for showing up on your doorstep, Celia. I'll see myself out.'

Which was the end of that, so why, she wondered, as she waited to hear the shop door slam before treading quietly downstairs, did she feel a certain disappointment? Was it because, for reasons she couldn't explain, he'd sparked an interest in her even though that interest was one hundred per cent inappropriate? Even though he was just the sort of guy she personally didn't like? Work-oriented, tough and way too arrogant and self-assured?

It was a relief she wouldn't be seeing him again. She didn't need to start questioning the choices she had made. She was perfectly content to keep her distance until the right guy came along. She was older and wiser now.

Leandro pulled to kerb, killed the engine of his Range Rover and, for a few seconds, he reclined in the seat, eyes narrowed on the bank of terraced houses on the opposite side of the narrow street. His car was wedged between a skip and an e-scooter that appeared to have been abandoned in haste, and it occurred to him that, in his rapid climb up the greasy pole of success, he had almost forgotten what the world on the other side of the tracks looked like.

A thin fall of snow had begun hours earlier and was trying hard to gather pace.

Finding out where Celia lived had been a piece of cake. He could have used one of his people to find out, but that felt like a distasteful invasion of privacy. Instead, he had gone to the shop and one of her assistants had been more than happy to provide the information. And why not? His ex-fiancée had been one of their biggest clients. Why would they withhold information?

That had been a day and a half ago.

He could have bypassed Celia and just headed up to Scotland himself, but with a man involved...

Things had become complicated, far more complicated than Leandro could ever have predicted when he and Julie had embarked on their joint plan to save her father from penury while salvaging his pride in the process.

He owed Charles more than money could buy and this had been his way of repaying the debt to the best of his ability.

And Julie, who had left her first marriage and had resolved never to go there again, had seen the sense of their arrangement.

But love?

Was that what had happened?

Leandro found it incomprehensible. What was the point of a learning curve if you didn't learn from it? Julie had been embittered by her first awful marriage. Why would she want to test the waters again when it came to her emotions?

Leandro was proud of his resolute stance when it came to harnessing all emotion. He could value the love he had for his father, mingled as it was with pity for the chances he had never taken because he had allowed the past to dictate his future. He could appreciate the depth of affection he had for Charles, who had been instrumental in helping him in his education. But he couldn't begin to understand, particularly after a bruising experience at the hands of someone else, why anyone would want to voluntarily go there again.

He, thankfully, had been smart enough to make sure he'd protected himself from the folly of losing his head to any woman and he was genuinely puzzled as to Julie's abrupt departure from lessons learnt.

Celia's enthusiastic and admiring descriptions of her brother as someone who scorned the trappings of routine and preferred the call of adventure had got every pore in Leandro's body bristling with justified scepticism, and the very view of this row of terraced houses staring at him now should have consolidated the suspicion that here were a likely pair of con artists, but no.

Something about Celia, something about the honesty in those amazing green eyes, had opened a door to the notion that she might just be right.

Julie might well and truly have fallen in love. Or else, *thought* she had fallen in love.

Which would scupper all their well-made plans to help her father, to rescue him from the financial bind now wrapped around him like tentacles.

But that was not why he was here, important though it was to at least try and find out what exactly was going on and find a way to a solution by hook or by crook.

He was here…because fate had decided to lend a very unhelpful hand.

With a sigh, Leandro slid out of the car and felt the sting of bitter cold working its way through his jeans and jumper and cashmere coat.

The house where she lived was neat, the tiny front garden tidy. They all were. There were lights on inside and he wondered what he might have done had she not been in. Driven a couple of blocks and then returned,

he presumed, but in this weather it was a relief that he wouldn't have to, and he banged
on the knocker, two raps, and waited.

From nowhere, he had a vivid image in his
head of her—those expressive green eyes, the
freckles, the riot of red hair, unrestrained, no
pretence at elegance. He closed his eyes for
a few seconds, feeling the stir of something
inside him he didn't want to identify.

He was hardly starved of sex. He had had
one very discreet and short-lived relationship
on a three-month stint in New York while he
and Julie had been engaged, for theirs was
to be a respectful but sexless union, and sensible rules had been put in place for obvious
reasons.

But all of a sudden, his libido had kicked
into gear and, just as fast, Leandro put
the brakes on that. With all inappropriate thoughts swiftly uprooted at source, he
lounged against the doorframe and waited.

It was a little after six. Snow was falling outside and Celia, barricaded in her cocoon of
warmth, was guiltily relieved that she wasn't
going anywhere, even though she should have
been, really, because it was Saturday night
and she was young, free and single.

Plus, after that nerve-wracking encounter

with Leandro, she had started thinking that she had to do something, had to venture into the world of dating, of finding someone.

The fact that he had managed to get under her skin the way he had had been a bit of a wake-up call.

If a guy like him, someone who did not meet any of the internal checks she had in place when it came to the opposite sex, could *get to her*, then something had to be done.

Very soon.

When the weather improved, she had resolved, gently turning down the offer of an evening out with the girls she worked with.

Who wanted to tramp through the snow to get to a crowded bar in Soho for drinks?

At least for this one evening, she had been very happy to stay in. So the sharp peal of her doorbell was annoying and, while she contemplated ignoring it, she stuck on her bedroom slippers and padded out to get it.

She was programmed never to ignore someone at the front door. When you spent all your formative years in the countryside where everyone knew everyone else, you never let your doorbell ring without answering it, and old habits died hard.

The last person Celia expected to find standing outside was Leandro Diaz and as she looked up and up and up, until their eyes met, she felt the breath leave her in a rush, felt the world narrow down to just him, tall, dark and stupidly handsome.

He was wearing black jeans and a black jumper, visible under the open lapels of a tan cashmere coat, and had a black scarf round his neck. He looked ridiculously elegant and very, very expensive and all those things flashed through her mind before the more prosaic thought… *What on earth was he doing on her doorstep?*

'What are you doing here?'

'I've done it again, haven't I?' Leandro said apologetically. 'Shown up unannounced on your doorstep. My apologies. I would have telephoned to warn you of my arrival, but I had a vague suspicion that you might have taken steps to avoid seeing me and I really had no choice but to see you.'

'You *had* to see me?' Celia belatedly remembered that he had accused her and her brother of being gold diggers and, now that the shock was wearing off, she resuscitated the anger she had felt at the insult. 'And you're damn right I would have taken steps to avoid you! In case you've forgotten, you accused Dan of targeting Julie for her money. You implied that I might have had a hand in it!' She remained firmly planted by the half-opened door, barring entry. She had every right to be furious at him showing up and invading her personal space *again*, but instead she felt a heat coursing through her that had nothing to do with anger. The same intense physical awareness that had gripped her two days ago was squeezing tightly now again.

Was it because it was such a novel sensation? She had cared deeply for Martin but, even in the height of their teenage romance, she had not felt anything like this, had not been *aware* of him as a living, breathing, *sexy* male...not like this.

Lack of experience, she told herself urgently. She glared at him with barely disguised hostility, but she had to force herself not to let her disobedient eyes rove down the length of his body.

'How did you find me, anyway?' she demanded.

'Celia, I simply went to your shop and asked one of your assistants. Considering my relationship with Julie, she didn't think that dispensing the information was beyond the pale, and why should she?

'Please let me in and I'll answer whatever questions you have.' Leandro looked briefly around him. 'It's freezing out here.'

He scanned her, taking in the bedroom slippers, the light jogging bottoms, the baggy cotton jumper, clothes that weren't designed for long conversations conducted outside in freezing conditions.

'What more do we have to say to one another?'

'I've located Julie and your brother.'

'You've *found them*?' Had he come, the bearer of bad tidings? Had they been in an accident? He had the information he had come to her for, he'd managed to find out where they were, so why was he here now if it wasn't to deliver news she didn't want to hear? News that could only be imparted face to face? That could only herald bad news. It was on a par with the phone that rang in the early hours of the morning. Celia fell back, allowing him to sweep past her. The small hallway seemed to shrink to the size of a matchbox as he turned to face her.

'Are they okay?' she asked tersely. 'Has there been some sort of terrible accident? Are they...?' Her mouth trembled and she blinked, while worst-case scenarios had a field day in her head.

'Alive and well,' Leandro interrupted hurriedly to prevent what looked like a descent into just the sort of emotionalism that was alien to him and unwelcome. 'To the best of my knowledge. The last purchase made was the day before yesterday and it's safe to say that they're en route to my house in Scotland.' He looked at her warily and she shot him a narrow-eyed, baleful and accusatory look from under her lashes.

'In which case, why scare the living daylights out of me?'

'Come again?'

'If you've managed to find them both and they're fine and dandy, then why come here and lead me to believe that there was something wrong?'

'Did I do that?'

'I suppose I should offer you tea or coffee now that you're here.' She propelled herself towards the kitchen, acutely aware of the smallness of the house and annoyed with herself for wondering what he might be thinking of his surroundings.

Following in her wake, Leandro vaguely noted what was around him. It was a small house painted in uniformly bland colours but the prints on the walls were quirky covers of old Parisian fashion magazines, nicely framed, and as he glanced to one side he saw through the semi-opened door a wooden mannequin being used as a frame for a half-

finished wedding dress and an easel on which
a large sheet of paper was clipped—presumably a picture of what the dress in progress
was destined to look like.

He paused, pushed open the door and
stepped inside, curiosity taking him towards
the easel to look at the drawing, and he turned
around when she angrily asked him what he
thought he was doing and how *dared he* make
himself at home in her house.

'You're very talented,' he commented, ignoring the heightened colour in her cheeks
and the spitting fire in her eyes and the hands
placed squarely on her hips.

'You can't just come in here and nose
around!'

She began moving towards the easel but
he beat her to it to stand in front of the ac-
complished drawing, one hand resting on the
paper so that she couldn't flip it away.

'Is this one of your commissions?'

Celia wanted the ground to open and swal-
low her up. He was being complimentary, but
she was too aware of him, too sensitive to
his overpowering personality and too conscious of the fact that he wasn't *a friend paying her a visit* to appreciate the compliment.
She could barely think straight as she stared
up at him. His eyes were so dark and so deep

that she had to fight a drowning sensation. Somewhere at the back of her mind, she knew that he was the sort of guy to find this extreme reaction amusing and she made an effort to put things in perspective.

'Yes,' she said tightly.

'Did you think up the design?'

'Yes.' She lowered her eyes and was aware of her laboured breathing. Her heart was beating like a sledgehammer and she folded her arms and took a step back. 'Edith wanted something a little more severe, but I managed to persuade her otherwise. She didn't have the figure for the style she was after and as soon as she saw what I had in mind, she was thrilled.' She shot him a look from under her lashes, expecting boredom and finding interest.

'I know Julie loved what you did.'

'Even though she won't be wearing it,' Celia muttered, brought back to reality after that short breathless moment when time seemed to have done weird things as he'd gazed down at her. 'Perhaps we could continue this conversation in the kitchen... Mr... er... Leandro. You can tell me what you're doing here and then you can be on your way.'

'Plans for the evening?' Leandro asked conversationally as she spun round on her heel and began heading out of the room, making sure, he noted, to firmly shut the door to her study behind her.

Celia was very glad he couldn't see her face as she shrugged, her back to him, and casually told him that it had been a long week.

'So...'

'Coffee would be good. Black. No sugar. I told Julie's father about the development with your brother. He'd been as much in the dark about what was happening as I was when I showed up at your shop two days ago. I thought it was only fair that he not cling to any unrealistic hopes about last-minute nerves. The last thing I wanted was for him to be under any illusions that Julie might materialise out of thin air just in the nick of time.'

Celia looked at him in silence, her head tilted thoughtfully to one side.

'You love him, don't you?'

'Love isn't a word that exists in my vocabulary.' Leandro flushed darkly and looked away. 'But yes, I happen to be very fond of him.'

'What did he say?' *Why was love a word that didn't exist in his vocabulary?*

'That's the problem.' Leandro waited until there was a mug of coffee in front of him, waited until she was sitting opposite him, waited until the silence started to become borderline oppressive. She didn't try and hurry him into an explanation, for which he was grateful because he was still processing the situation himself. 'Yesterday I received a call that Charles has been admitted to hospital with a stroke.'

He looked away. Celia saw the tic beating in his tightly clenched jaw and the rigid stillness of his posture and she reached out to place her hand gently on his arm.

'It's not your fault. I mean, for telling him.'

Their eyes met as he firmly pulled his arm out of reach.

'I don't believe I said anything about it being my fault, did I?' But he rose to his feet to restlessly pace the kitchen before sitting back down.

'No, you didn't,' Celia murmured.

'I've come because I need to tell Julie what's happening, and I need to try and persuade her to revise whatever plans she's making with your brother. Or at least to work with me at finding a place where she can temper the truth for the sake of her father's health. I… I judge that it would be a more successful trip if you were there with me to likewise talk to your brother.'

'You want me to…'

'Come to Scotland with me. It would be a matter of a night or two, at the very most.'

'No!'

'I would make it worth your while financially.'

'Do you honestly think that you can get whatever you want by throwing money around?'

Leandro shot her a thin smile. 'You'd be shocked at how often it works.'

'Absolutely not!' She fidgeted in the chair, stood up, walked towards the kitchen window to peer out at the tiny darkened back patio overlooked by a bank of houses just beyond the border of her fence. When she swung back round to face him, it was to find his eyes pinned to her with a mixture of strange hesitancy and reluctant resignation.

'There's more to it than that,' he said quietly. 'Of course, it's vitally important that Julie know about her father's state of health, vitally important that he doesn't have any continued stress that might exacerbate his situation…and perhaps you'll change your mind about Scotland when I tell you what my marriage to Julie was really all about…'

CHAPTER THREE

LEANDRO GRIMACED. CONFIDING was not in his nature. In fact, it was so much *not* in his nature that he was temporarily at a loss as to where to begin.

Her eyes were curious, her mouth parted and there was a puzzled expectancy in her expression. Of course there was. She was an incurable romantic. It shone in everything she said and in her sympathetic misconception that he was somehow broken-hearted, having been dumped by his ex.

On every level, she was unknown territory. Leandro had always made sure to steer clear of women with romantic dreams because he knew that he was incapable of fulfilling them. The thought of becoming entangled with someone who wanted more than he could give brought him out in a cold sweat. A woman in search of love had no place in his life. His speciality was an ability to shower lavish gifts and open doors to experiences only afforded to the uber rich.

But she deserved to have the full story because he needed her co-operation and it was unfair to keep her in the dark, that being the case.

'You think that Julie and I are…in love…'

'I don't know. I did, to start with, but I'm beginning to think that maybe that wasn't the case. But if that's so, then why would you get married in the first place?' She frowned. 'I know that you two go back a long way…'

Leandro could see her trying to work out how anyone could make a leap from friendship to marriage without the middleman of *Love* being at the party.

Looking at her now, Leandro suddenly felt a hundred years old. There had been no gullible staging posts in his life. He had made the leap from boy to man at a young age. Too young? He'd never asked himself that question. He'd grown up associating love with pain and loss. He'd never hankered for kids because he knew his limitations and respected them. Love wasn't for him and if you couldn't give love then surely any child would be born immediately disadvantaged?

'Many would agree that a solid friendship is the best basis for a successful union,' he now said, curtly. 'The statistics say it all. Most marriages end in divorce once the shine wears off and reality begins to bite. People walk up the aisle with stars in their eyes but give it a few years and the stars get snuffed out and the next joint venture out is to the divorce courts.'

'That's an awful interpretation of marriage!'

'We'll have to agree to disagree on that one. The point I'm making is that Julie and I had…an understanding. I'm assuming you know about her first marriage?'

'Yes, she mentioned that it wasn't a happy one.'

'We made a joint decision to marry for practical reasons.'

'Children?' Celia asked faintly.

'No.' Leandro paused and marvelled that spelling out the blunt facts behind their marriage, which he had not once questioned to himself, now felt like an act of positive cruelty. Impatient with himself, he shook his head and frowned. 'What we were going to have would have been, essentially, an open marriage.'

'An *open marriage*…'

'There's no need to sound so shocked,' Leandro said irritably.

'But I *am* shocked,' Celia said simply. 'And I don't understand…'

'Julie found out several months ago that her father had, basically, gone bankrupt. She made the discovery quite by accident. Happened to be at home at their estate in Northumberland when her father's bank manager unexpectedly decided to pay a visit. Charles was out but Julie managed to glean sufficient information to form a rough idea of what was going on. Mountains of debt…and a supply chain to his outlets that had ground to a halt because suppliers were owed money.' Leandro sighed and raked his fingers through his hair. 'I could go into the details of when what happened and what the knock-on effects were, but, to sum it up, he was in deep financial trouble with creditors banging on the door and threats of the family estate having to be dismantled to pay debts.'

'How awful,' Celia said softly. 'Where do *you* fit in, if you don't mind me asking?'

'I…' Leandro paused. So much of his life was accessible and out there on the World Wide Web, the bare bones of the road he had travelled to get from A to B, but this? No, this was a part of him that had always been firmly barricaded behind No Trespass signs.

His thoughts and feelings about the life he'd
led and the debts he owed.

'Yes?' Celia prompted. He didn't like talking about himself. He was intensely private
and she could tell that parting with whatever
information he thought she was owed was
going to be difficult. She got that. In a way.
She had never discussed the business of her
break-up with Martin with anyone. She had
smiled and offered anodyne explanations, but
she had largely kept her feelings private.

The fact that he felt obliged to open up with
her, more than anything else, showed her just
how much he wanted her to go to Scotland
with him because Dan was there and suddenly, because of that, she had become part
of the equation.

'When I said that Julie and I go back a
long way, I should clarify by adding that our
fathers…grew up together in a manner of
speaking…'

'What does that mean? In a manner of
speaking?' She felt as though she were being
asked to swim through a river of treacle to get
to what he was trying to say. 'You grew up…
in…'

'Argentina.' He sighed, fidgeted and then

muttered, lowering his eyes, 'I don't make a habit of doing this.'

'Confiding?'

'All that touchy-feely stuff normally has no place in my life...but in this instance...'

Just for a split second, there was something so incredibly *human* about him that Celia was shaken.

'My father worked on a ranch for a guy called Roberto Suarez. He was a dogsbody, but he became close to Roberto's son, Fernando, and then, along the way, with Julie's father, who had been to university in Oxford with Fernando and used to come over to the ranch for the long summer vacations. They were all roughly the same age. They hung out. My father was an excellent horseman and I suppose they bonded over that.'

He shrugged. When he was much younger, Leandro had been scathing about the quality of this so-called friendship, which he saw as one based on pity because how could the masters ever feel anything meaningful towards the servant? But time had proved him wrong and he had never really forgiven himself for that brief period of resentment. He'd been young.

'When my mother...was no longer around...

they took my father under their wing, so to speak, and much later, as the years rolled on…well, my father had an accident. He was thrown from a horse and was bedridden for a time. When it transpired that he was not going to be able to work in the capacity he'd worked in previously, Fernando, who was now in charge of the ranch and with a family of his own, ensured that my father was secure in his house…'

'And where were you at the time? Did your mother…pass on?'

'My mother passed on or, should I say, continued her onward journey in life with a very rich house guest who had visited the ranch to talk business with Roberto Suarez. She never looked back. I was a toddler at the time.' Leandro moved on quickly from that statement of fact even though, as he looked at her, there was a gentleness in her gaze that almost made him want to break the rulebook and elaborate. He didn't, of course. Not his thing.

'When my father had his fall… Roberto gave him, as I said, permanent residence at the place he had always called home and Julie's father…took care of every aspect of my education. He paid for me to attend a private school in Buenos Aires. My father had been saving for years but the accident reduced his income. It was a mess, as I came to understand. Later, Charles took care of every single bill that came my way, when I gained a scholarship to study at Cambridge. During the holidays, he paid for my flights back to Argentina and when I wasn't there, I stayed at his country house, sometimes for weeks on end.'

'It's how you know Julie…'

'Correct. We met from a young age but became good friends once I began studying in England. I was at her wedding, as it happens. I was the first and only person she told about her father's financial situation. I would have been happy to have simply handed over the cash to sort out the mess but he's too damned proud for his own good…'

There was affection, indulgence and frustration in Leandro's voice.

'I get it,' Celia said softly. 'You and Julie decided on a marriage of convenience to bail her father out without him seeing it as an act of charity.'

'Charles fondly thinks that he's giving me the cachet of being absorbed into one of the country's oldest families. He doesn't know that I don't give a damn about any of that.'

'But what about love?'

Leandro shrugged. 'What does that have to do with anything? I'm repaying a debt, doing what any man of honour would do. There's no place in this scenario for misty-eyed day-dreams.' He leant forward with a sense of urgency. 'This is why I've come here. Of course, I can't drag you off to Scotland with me. But I think that if for some reason Julie fancies herself in love with your brother, the two of us together might stand a better chance of at least trying to find a way to salvage the situation.'

'I barely know you,' Celia said, without thinking, and his eyebrows shot up in obvious amusement.

'What do you think I'm going to do?'

'Nothing!' But she was bright red. 'But...the thought of just taking off with a stranger...'

'I wouldn't ask if I didn't think it was important. Charles is in hospital with a stroke. Not only will Julie's disappearance be a major cause of worry for him, but he will now be having to come to terms with the fact that he might be looking at losing everything that has been in his family for centuries. Either that, or he, as you put it, accepts charity from me, which would cut to the quick for a man who is kind and generous but too proud for his own good.'

'Yes, I get that...'

'You're one hundred per cent safe with me,' Leandro said earnestly, and Celia felt as though, somehow, he had a direct hotline to her thoughts and was having a private laugh at her unfounded misgivings. Not that she wasn't well aware that her misgivings were unfounded, but she had led a sheltered life where impulse had always taken a back seat to common sense and it was hard not to fall back into that mindset even though she could see where he was coming from.

Dan had been the impulsive one. He had been the one who lived outside the box, always willing to take risks and explore options.

Celia, on the other hand, several years younger and born after her mother had suffered two miscarriages, had been raised with kid gloves, protected by loving parents who no longer had the mindset to let her run wild and free, as they had her brother.

That was the only basis for her hesitancy, she feverishly told herself.

The fact that there was a treacherous sizzle of something disturbing in her responses to this man had nothing to do with anything.

'Celia...'

'I'm not suggesting anything...it's the way I am... I suppose I'm quite a careful person...' She fell into an erratic explanation for her reluctance before lapsing into silence, mesmerised by the dark eyes pinned to her face as he listened to her rambling.

'You're not my type.'

'I beg your pardon?'

'I'm not being at all...insulting when I tell you that you're perfectly safe with me because you're not my type.'

Celia was mortified. She had no idea how to respond to the bluntness of his statement, and the fact that he genuinely hadn't said it to offend her, because she could see the gentle sincerity in his eyes, somehow made his casual remark all the more offensive. Yes, she was short with freckles that had once been the bane of her life, but it still hurt to have her physical shortcomings pointed out by a guy with killer looks.

By *anybody* it would have been bad enough, but with someone as devastatingly good-looking as Leandro, it was positively humiliating.

'I realise I'm not a catwalk model,' Celia began stiffly, and Leandro grinned and waved his hand in airy dismissal.

'Nothing to do with looks,' he asserted. 'You're a romantic, Celia. Am I right? You don't really understand why I would want to get married for any reason other than love.'

'I see why you feel indebted to Julie's father,' Celia stammered, still red-faced but slightly mollified by what he had just said.

'But for you, marriage is something that goes hand in hand with love. For me? I have no such illusions, and when I say that you're not my type? My type of women aren't looking for permanence, at least not with me. Scotland will involve a helicopter flight and then two nights at my estate, where your brother and Julie are currently hiding out.'

'How do you know for sure?'

'Because Julie has a key and it's the only place they are likely to be heading. Trust me on this.' He looked around him and then said, as though the thought had only just occurred to him, 'I haven't asked, but I'm assuming that you would be able to take two days off from your commitments?'

'Work?'

'I was thinking of commitments of a more personal nature. Boyfriend? Girlfriend? No dogs at any rate...'

'I...no, I don't have a boyfriend,' Celia said stiffly. 'Not that that's any of your business.'

'It is if I think it's something that might influence your decision.'

'I would never go out with someone who's autocratic enough to disapprove of me being away for a couple of days.'

'With another man. Apologies, forgot we'd established that I don't fall into that category.' Leandro grinned but then said, seriously, thoughtfully, 'You'll be gone for two days at the very most and I would want to leave first thing in the morning. I can't force you to accept any financial compensation from me for the inconvenience, but every year I get several tickets for front seats at the London Fashion week. This year, it's a winter spectacular according to the blurb.'

'You like that kind of thing?' She knew that he was cleverly tempting her in a way that showed just how adept he was at getting what he wanted. Would she want to go to the show of the year for a dress designer? Just thinking about the chance made her feel faint.

'Oh, I try to avoid that event at all costs,' he murmured silkily, 'but I imagine the opportunities for you could be considerable. I could even put a word in about your…er… designs—from what I've seen, you've got a great deal of talent, which could end up going to waste without the right exposure.'

'Are you trying to bribe me?'

'I'm trying to persuade you.'

'Will you let me think about it?'

Leandro smiled slowly and sat back. 'Of course. The last thing I would want to do is force your hand. I'll call you...' he glanced at his Rolex then looked at her '...in precisely two hours.'

He would send a car for her and it would deliver her to an airfield, where he would meet her shortly after lunch.

Celia had squashed her apprehensions and agreed. She'd been swayed by her conscience. If someone were to suffer a misfortune because of her, then how would she ever be able to live with herself? If Julie's father, on the brink of financial collapse, were to suffer a fatal stroke through the sheer stress of the situation, then no amount of reasoning would have persuaded her to conclude that walking away from the situation had been okay.

She also wanted to find out what was going on with Dan. Leandro's assumption was that if anyone was going to be hurt, it would be Julie for having been targeted by someone who was after her money. Money she didn't have, as things stood. Was he still of the opinion that her brother was guilty of being a gold digger? The topic had been shelved. He'd decided that he needed her input and so had tactfully pulled back from anything contentious.

From Celia's point of view, what if her brother was the one at risk of being hurt if Julie had absconded because of a sudden attack of to-be-expected pre-wedding nerves? What if she had second thoughts and decided to get back together with Leandro? There were compelling reasons for her to do just that and where would that leave Dan? Footloose and easy-going he might be, but, like her, he was a solid traditionalist at heart. He'd been out with countless girls, but he'd never come close to asking any of them to marry him. What if *the one* turned out to be a mistake? She could remember her own hurt all those years ago when the blinkers had been pulled from her eyes and she wouldn't wish that on her brother.

And then the dangling carrot of that ticket to the fashion show...

He'd known just how to tempt. He'd been smart enough to drop all talk of money changing hands and instead had offered her something priceless. A golden opportunity to climb the career ladder and to see, first hand, what was happening in the fashion world, to have a possible audience for her calling cards.

They stood on opposite sides of the fence on pretty much everything. He was cold, tough and driven to make money and she could never like a guy like that, but she'd agreed, and even if the misgivings hadn't been completely put to bed she managed to put a lid on them as, the following afternoon, she was duly delivered to the airfield in gathering gloom.

The helicopter was a dark shadow against the velvety sky, as still and as ominous as a giant, watchful, waiting insect.

Snow had gathered apace overnight though not enough to settle. The chauffeur-driven car slowly pulled to a stop just as the door to the helicopter was flung open and there he was, a commanding silhouette, barely visible in the semi darkness.

She had her overnight bag with her, stuffed with thick clothing and a selection of thermals and her computer in its waterproof case. Now, as the driver fought the sleet and snow to open the car door, Celia took a couple of seconds to review her situation. The darkness and Leandro's commanding presence didn't do much for her nervous system, which suddenly went into sharp overdrive.

Her heart began a steady thump as she headed towards the helicopter, with the driver bringing up the rear with her cases.

If she'd ever secretly mourned the predictability of her day-to-day life, then no one could accuse her of not being wildly and scarily unpredictable now.

'Good. On time.'

The helicopter door slammed behind her. She'd never been in a helicopter before. Her life didn't include such adventures.

Just the two of them in a tiny little bubble with sleet and flurries of snow gusting around them.

She was shaking as he strapped her in but, even though she was in a state of anxious meltdown, her eyes skittered to him. He was in black, from his shoes to his black polo neck and the bomber jacket. Like her, he was wearing a woolly hat, which he kept on. It was freezing in the helicopter.

'You're scared,' he threw over his shoulder, before opening the throttle so that the eerie silence turned into a cacophony of noise from the rotor blades. 'Don't be,' he shouted. 'You're in safe hands.'

But Celia felt far from safe as the helicopter spun into motion, accelerating sharply upwards and then buzzing at speed over a vista submerged in darkness.

She hadn't thought out what she was going to say to her brother when she saw him and she couldn't think about that now because she was too busy clinging to her seat, eyes tightly shut, breathing all over the place.

Through a haze of fear, she was aware of the helicopter shuddering like a tin can in a tornado, taking for ever, and then the descent, sharp and fast and over in the blink of an eye.

The silence as the rotor blades slowed was as deafening as the noise of them rotating had been.

She opened her eyes to find that Leandro had unbuckled and moved towards her and was grinning.

'Have you had your eyes closed for the entire flight?'

Busying herself with the safety belt, Celia glanced at him and blushed.

'It's my first time in a helicopter,' she muttered. 'How did I know that it wasn't going to crash?'

'Because I was piloting it,' Leandro said with supreme confidence. 'It's pretty bad here. Leave your bags. I'll take them. We can make a dash for the house. Snow here isn't like snow in London. Up here, I find the snow is generally a little less polite.'

'I know,' Celia puffed breathlessly, 'it's the same in Shropshire where I grew up. It comes and then never knows when it's time to leave.'

'Well put. Let me help you.' He cranked open the door to a white, barren and starkly beautiful wilderness.

For a few seconds, Celia looked out in awe at the splendid isolation. Pure darkness encased a wintry wonderland that shimmered under silent, falling snow. She forgot how cold she was, how anxious, how apprehensive. Dark shapes were visible, definitions of the landscape, but they could have landed on another planet.

The snow was thick and vicious, slicing through her clothes as he hoisted the various bags in one hand and propelled her through the darkness towards the looming vast shape of his country estate.

She could *sense* unease in his silence.

They hit the front door at pace. Massive front door. Behind them, the helicopter was a disappearing dark blot and behind that, Celia could only surmise, lay gates and trees and hedges and who knew what else. All the stuff of a country estate.

The actual manor house was so big as they

stood in front of it that Celia could barely see where it began and ended through the densely falling snow.

It was shrouded in complete darkness and as they entered, Leandro banging on the lights, flooding the vast hall with light, bitterly cold.

He dumped all the bags and made straight through the hall, bypassing the grand staircases to the left and the right and towards the bowels of the house.

Celia followed. She had to half run because he was moving at a brisk pace but, even so, she still managed to take in the opulent grandeur of the surroundings. Pale walls, marble, exquisite panelling and chandeliers and paintings that looked as though they cost a fortune.

There was an urgency to his purposeful stride that ratcheted up her nervousness and, sure enough, when he flung open a cupboard to fire up the central heating and turned to her, she knew what he was going to say before the words could leave his mouth.

'There's no one here.'

Their eyes tangled and a frisson swept through her body as the ramifications of that simple statement took root.

No Dan. No Julie. No safety net of other people around, however thorny the atmosphere might have been. Just her and Leandro rattling around in his sprawling mansion with a snowstorm raging outside. One night here? Two? Or more?

As he'd said, the snow in this part of the world, as it was in Shropshire, was not polite. It didn't fall for a couple of hours before packing it in. It outstayed its welcome.

What did that mean? What if they were stuck here?

Celia didn't want to dwell on worst-case scenarios but as she stood there, in front of him, they filled her head, swamping all rational thought until she could feel her pulses racing and her body prickling with panicked perspiration.

She was as safe as houses with him, whatever the circumstances. She wasn't his type and he wasn't hers.

But those killer looks...

She could breathe him in, the smell of cold mingled with woody aftershave. It made her feel unsteady on her feet and she automatically took a couple of steps back, breathing in deeply and gathering herself.

'If they're not here, then where are they? You said that they were going to be here!'

'It's obvious they started in this direction.' He began walking, throwing over his shoulder that she should follow him, that there was no harm in checking all the rooms. 'But...' he picked up where he had left off as he led the way up one of the grand staircases, which ascended to a huge galleried landing '...with the last leg to go and travelling by car, they must have decided not to brave the weather.'

'So what do we do now?' Celia dashed past him and then spun round so that she was ahead of him, looking down the staircase to the marble-floored landing and the richness of the paintings on the walls. From this vantage point she was almost on eye level with him and for a few seconds she regretted her move because they were so close, close enough to see the flecks of gold in his midnight-dark eyes and the lush thickness of his lashes. She breathed in sharply, heart beating like a sledgehammer.

'We check all the rooms and then decide in the morning.'

'Is that *it*?' Celia cried.

'What more is it possible to do at this hour in the evening? There's no way I'm going to attempt to make the journey back in this weather.' His eyes were as cool as his voice. 'I'm not jeopardising your life nor am I jeopardising my own because you're panicking about being here with me.'

'That's not it *at all*!'

'You're tired and hungry, but getting over-emotional about this situation isn't going to help either of us.'

'And what if we're stuck here for longer than one night?' Celia demanded. 'Will you be able to fly the helicopter back in the morning if it continues to snow overnight?'

Leandro met her blazing green eyes with a remote, unreadable expression.

Her cheeks were flushed, her copper hair tangled around her heart-shaped face, her full lips pursed. She oozed fury. How could that be attractive? It couldn't. He loathed this sort of extreme emotionalism. What was the point of overreacting to something that couldn't be changed? And yet, as he stared at her, he was disconcerted by the tug of something strong, swift and primal. She was the very essence of lush, tempting femininity and as he looked away, impatient with his response to her, he could feel a telltale tic in his jaw, a potent reminder that his lofty reassurances that she was utterly safe with him might have a few holes he hadn't foreseen.

But a lifetime of iron control came to his rescue. He had never been ruled by his body and that was something that was never going to change.

'Pointless question,' he said smoothly, moving to step past her, feeling the warmth of her body close to his as he brushed past and sensing the hurried, breathless shift of her body to let him pass by. Now, he was gazing down at her, her face upturned to his, and again, that uninvited intrusion of a libido that was always kept under control. 'In the morning, we'll see what's happening with the weather and take it from there. For now, I'll show you where you can sleep, and we'll have something to eat. Tomorrow, as I've said, is another day.'

CHAPTER FOUR

HOW WAS LEANDRO to know that those glibly spoken words that *'tomorrow is another day'* would come back to bite him? Tomorrow *should* have been another day. It should have been the day they returned to London, where he would pick up the search for Julie, having first begun the business of sorting her father's financial woes, never mind about the old man's misplaced pride. He and Celia would part company, she the better for tickets to the fashion show. Despite what he had said to Celia, he had been privately convinced that, with no Julie or Dan there, making the trip back by helicopter the following day would have been a certainty.

That was four days ago.

He knew that when snow fell in this part of the world, it meant business. He had awoken to the silent force of a snowstorm the morning after they'd arrived and realised that any hope of getting the helicopter up was out of the question.

In his meticulously ordered life, where there was no place for surprises, the weather had decided to blindside him.

They had sat opposite one another at the vast table in his kitchen, which was a marvel of what money could buy, from the four-door cream oven to the high-tech seldom-used gadgets and he had seen exactly what she'd been thinking as clearly as if her thoughts had been emblazoned across her forehead in neon lettering.

Get me out of here.

She couldn't have looked more horrified if she'd glanced up to discover that the sky was falling down.

She'd been prepared to be polite for a night or two, knowing that she would be rescued from having to be alone with him because they would be greeted at the house by Julie and her brother.

The prospect of them both sharing space for longer than that without any convenient chaperones or a helicopter on red-alert standby had appalled her and she hadn't bothered to disguise her reaction, even though he had spent at least an hour assuring her that the house was so vast that they could get lost in it and, besides, he would remove himself during the day to carry on working from the office that was set up in another wing of the manor house.

'You won't notice I'm here,' he had said. 'We can meet in the evenings for dinner, but you'll find your quarters comfortable enough for you to stay put all day while we're here. You'll have your own suite, with a television and a dedicated space if you want to work…'

'Good,' she had said with visible relief, and so here they were, several days later, their time together reduced to an hour or so in the evenings over dinner.

Where he had always had a short attention span when it came to listening to people talk about their feelings, he found, to his intense irritation, that her silence on the subject got on his nerves. Where he was used to zoning out, his mind veering off to work-related issues when meandering anecdotes from dates turned into searching questions designed to elicit confidences he had no intention of sharing, he found himself encouraging her to open up. Thus far his success rate hovered around the zero mark.

And in this scenario, how was it possible that his libido moved into fifth gear every time he looked at her? How did that even begin to make sense?

Was it the novelty of being in the company of a woman who didn't spare him a second glance? Or did those lush curves appeal to him in ways that bypassed his brain and went straight to his groin?

Or maybe it was just the stark isolation of their circumstances...

He banged his fist in seething frustration on the desk where he was now forced to abandon work because the Internet had decided to crash, and scowled.

It was a little after three in the afternoon. Through the window, the swirling snow against a darkening sky made for an eerie landscape.

There was an afternoon to fill and an evening to get through. For a workaholic, the prospect of idling in the slow lane indefinitely was the stuff of nightmares.

Defeated by the lack of Internet and not caring for the direction of his thoughts, Leandro vacated his office to wander in the direction of the kitchen.

The size of the place had naturally lent itself to subdivision, with one half reserved for friends and family as and when they chose to visit, which was not often, and the other half devoted to work-related gatherings, which had been far more frequent over the years.

It was not unusual for entire high-performing teams to be given all-expenses-paid time there where they could enjoy first-class service and idyllic surroundings with their family.

Connecting doors could slide seamlessly into place, separating one side from the other completely. It was a marvel of advanced engineering and Leandro had personally overseen its implementation.

Now, making his way through the vast house, absently contemplating the prospect of Celia and his wayward responses to her and wondering, yet again, what the hell was going on with him, he glanced through the windows of one of the rooms he swung by and there she was.

Outside!

What was she doing *outside*?

Was this what she got up to mid-afternoon when he was in the office, sitting in front of a computer, linked up to half the world for his uninterrupted hours of virtual meetings?

Having walks outside in driving snow? Or was this her first venture out to make a change from the horror of being cooped up in a luxury manor house the size of a small castle?

Leandro didn't give himself time to dwell. Instead, he sprinted to the front door, grabbing the house keys en route, not bothering to hunt down his wellies from the boot room behind the kitchen.

The freezing cold hit him with the force of a body blow. He gasped sharply but didn't slow his pace, moving swiftly through the snow and oblivious to the physical discomfort.

He could handle black runs in the most challenging of conditions and ergo he could handle anything.

Not least a stubborn woman who should know better than to put her life at risk by venturing out in hostile weather conditions!

He reached her at speed, aware of the slushing of the snow in his loafers and the bitter wind stinging his face.

She was so small against the vastness of the landscape, a vulnerable little dot, and he fought against an urge to pull her against him.

She was huddled into so many layers of clothing and her woolly hat was pulled low over her eyes and his heart clenched with a surge of protectiveness that took him by surprise.

He reached out to circle her arm with his

fingers, turning her to face him because she hadn't seen him approaching from behind her.

'What the hell do you think you're doing out there?'

The sudden fear and panic that had gripped him when he'd spotted her outside made him sound harsher than he'd intended. But he wasn't going to apologise because it was sheer crazy recklessness to be out in these conditions, where the darkness and the falling snow concealed a multitude of potential danger zones.

'What on earth are you doing?' Celia, alone with her thoughts and enjoying the peace of not being in the house where she seemed to be on constant alert to the sound of his approaching footsteps, stared at Leandro in astonishment.

Shouldn't he be working?

It was all he did! He worked from the early hours of the morning to late in the evening. Either he had a limitless amount of things that couldn't possibly be deferred for a day or two or else, more likely, he was intent on doing everything within his power to avoid her.

She couldn't blame him. Why would he want to be stuck out here with a woman who had come along for the ride as a matter of necessity?

This was the sort of wildly romantic place he would choose to come with a lover. She could picture him, the Lord of the Manor, with an icy beauty, strolling hand in hand through the ruggedly untamed countryside, stopping only to lose themselves in one another.

Instead, he'd found himself closeted with a woman he barely liked, reduced to small talk when it just couldn't be avoided.

Conscious of that fact and not wanting to be a bother, Celia had been at pains to be in his company as little as possible. They ate together and she was surprised that he was as good a cook as he was, turning down her offers to help because, surprisingly, he enjoyed it.

Watching and listening, enjoying the sight of him moving confidently around the well-equipped kitchen and knowing that her disobedient eyes were just fanning the flames of an illicit attraction that no amount of common sense could squash, Celia hung onto every word that left his lips.

She knew it was wrong. It wasn't as though he were sharing anything with her that he wouldn't have shared with anyone else who happened to be there at the time he just happened to be throwing a few things in a pan! She was very careful to keep herself to herself, which wasn't difficult because whenever she was around him, she became curiously tongue-tied. It had been easier to argue with him when he'd first shown up on her doorstep with his accusations and arrogant assumptions about her and Dan.

But out here, there had been a lull in hostilities, and she had been treacherously aware that, within the lull, she had glimpsed a multifaceted guy with a sharp sense of humour and a charm that she couldn't have predicted.

Not the kind of man who was her type, because their worlds were just so far apart, because she would always need someone so much more normal and down-to-earth. So she was as safe as houses on that front…but he was still so physically attractive that what woman wouldn't feel her insides go just a little bit squishy in his presence?

She tried to yank her arm free, sensitive to the heat pouring from him straight into her.

'I'm rescuing you,' Leandro gritted. He began tugging her back in the direction of the house and, rather than resist, she hurried alongside him because the force of the snow didn't permit extended arguments to be conducted outside. Not without hypothermia kicking in.

'Rescuing me?' she all but shouted once they were inside the house with the front door firmly shut against the elements. She'd leapt back and now she glared at him, hands on her hips, fuming green eyes clashing with equally fuming black ones. 'You were *rescuing* me?'

Leandro wondered what the world was coming to when an act of pure chivalry could be met with open hostility.

'Don't be bloody-minded,' he growled. 'Have you any idea just how dangerous it is attempting to venture out in this weather anywhere near that loch?'

'I *know* where the loch is, Leandro! I've been having an afternoon walk every day since we've been…been…cooped up here!'

'I get it this isn't exactly what you'd bought into!'

'Is it what *you've* bought into?'

'It could have been a damn sight worse.' Leandro was so aware of her pulsing, throbbing, sexily alluring feminine anger that he was driven to stare, knowing even as his eyes rested on her that what he *should* be doing was looking away. Cutting the conversation dead—if she wanted to berate him for being a gentleman, then that was her problem.

However, he couldn't tear his eyes away. She'd yanked off the woolly hat and he wanted to reach out and push her tangled hair away from her face, gather her into his arms and kiss her senseless.

No...he wanted to do more than that...he wanted to take her to his bed, see her naked, that wild hair strewn across his pillow...he wanted to touch...

'I wasn't in any danger.' Celia's voice hitched in her throat and she stumbled a couple of steps back.

'I could do without any more complications if you'd fallen in,' he muttered, looking away but only for a second. 'This is a pointless conversation.'

'I grew up where snow was something that happened once a year!' Celia snapped, patches of bright colour staining her cheeks. 'I know how to handle being in it! Which *you*,' she added, 'evidently do not!'

'Meaning?'

'*Meaning* that when you decided to do your knight-in-shining-armour routine and rescue the damsel in distress, you didn't stop to think that braving a snowstorm in some cotton track pants and a jumper and...and shoes without socks might not have been the best idea in the world!'

But he *had* played the knight in shining armour, hadn't he? And whatever he'd said about only rushing out to save her from her own carelessness because he didn't want the hassle of her breaking a leg on him, she *knew* that he had reacted on instinct. The instinct to protect someone he thought might have been in a vulnerable situation. That was who he was, whether he wanted to admit it or not, and when was the last time she had laid eyes on *any* knights in shining armour?

Celia knew that her one disappointing experience with Martin, her youthful mistake of being in love with the idea of being in love without the maturity to delve deeper into her headlong rush into an engagement with a guy she'd liked but not loved, had made her cautious, but had her retreat from the messy world of men and dating also made her cynical?

Leandro had been right when he'd told her that she was a romantic, that she wanted the whole fairy-tale happy-ever-after ending for herself.

But was that something she believed for herself because that was just the way she'd been brought up? Did she take the whole business of romance for granted because it was in her DNA to think that she would end up like her parents, in love after so many years, travelling down a straightforward road to a predictably happy destination?

In the meanwhile, had her feverish building of protective walls around herself gradually turned her into someone who had bit by bit been losing the ability to trust? Had holding all men at arm's length, while she waited for Mr Right to magically come along, curdled her natural softness into hard-baked cynicism?

It was easy to dwell on the marvels of True Love from a distance. If you never took risks, then you would never get hurt. Had she drifted towards that place? Safely marooned on her little island, all by herself? Prickly and incapable of just being *nice* to a guy who had hurtled out of this house because he'd thought she might have been in mortal danger?

Even if she was familiar with this sort of inclement weather a lot more than he was?

But he got to her...made her behave out of character...threw up her defences even though she knew she was being silly...

And he was savvy enough to figure out that she was prickly around him!

'I'm sorry,' she muttered, casting her eyes downwards even though her body language was still rigid with tension at the wayward direction of her thoughts. 'You rushed out because you thought I might have been in danger of hurting myself and I appreciate that.'

He didn't reply, instead spinning round on his heel and heading to the kitchen.

'I… I also didn't expect to see you,' she confessed, following him as he stripped off the soggy jumper to the tee shirt underneath.

'I'd better go and get into some dry clothes,' he said, turning to her and raking his fingers through his damp hair.

'You should.' Truce in place. Felt better. She might feel safer when she was angry with him, because that way she could shut the door on inappropriate reactions, but a truce felt better and she realised that, over the past few days, she had become accustomed to not arguing with him about the situation.

She'd grown used to the way he sometimes raised his eyebrows and half smiled when she dug her heels in and argued with him about something and nothing. She enjoyed the absent way he sometimes let slip things about himself without really realising it and the way he had of making her laugh, because, oddly for someone who could be so arrogant and autocratic, he was also very good at doing that.

'You'll get your death of a cold if you hang around for too long in wet clothes.'

'That's an old wives' tale.' But he glanced

down at his loafers, which he proceeded to kick off, as though only just remembering that his feet were wet. 'Never had a cold in my life.'

Their eyes collided and Celia drew in a shaky breath, which almost managed to clear her head but didn't quite seem to dispel the sudden flare of crackling tension that had sprung up from nowhere. Was it her imagination or was she reading something in the depths of those dark eyes, something that was thrilling and unsettling at the same time?

Or were her own contraband thoughts interfering with her common sense and making her sense something that wasn't there? She blinked and looked away but she knew that she was flushed and breathing fast.

'Internet's down.' Leandro broke the stretching silence and Celia breathed a sigh of relief at the normality of his remark, something to cling onto to distract her from her misbehaving mind.

'You're kidding. When did that happen?'

'A couple of hours ago. I tried to do as much as I could without it, but it was hopeless.'

'Is that how you managed to spot me outside?'

'I was heading towards the kitchen.'

They had, thankfully, managed to contact Julie via Facebook two days previously, to tell her about her father's condition, even though the conversation had been limited because of the Internet wherever they were falling in and out of service in the continuing poor weather. It had been Celia's idea because Leandro, to her surprise, was not connected on Facebook or interested in any other form of social media that could get an uninvited foothold into his private life.

'I guess you'll have to discover what life is like without being connected to the rest of the world via a computer.' Celia smiled a little shyly and he grinned back at her.

'You can tell me how you manage to make life work for you on that front when I'm back down,' he said drily, eyes still pinned to her face as he hovered by the door, on the verge of leaving but not managing to do so quite yet.

Celia broke the spell by turning away, telling him that she would make them some tea…there were some biscuits she'd spotted in one of the cupboards.

Only when he'd left the kitchen did she sag with relief. She made a pot of tea in a rush, every nerve in her body keyed up to hear him returning while she tried to think of what on earth he was going to do if the Internet remained down and the snow continued to layer everything in a blanket of white.

He still managed to surprise her when her back was turned as she searched through the cupboards for the biscuits. With no one in the place, there had been a shortage of fresh food easily compensated by freezers and larders bursting at the seams.

'So...' his lazy drawl had her spinning round to find him changed into a pair of faded jeans, tan loafers and a black tee shirt, for the massive house was incredibly warm, despite the conditions outside '...you were going to tell me how you busy yourself without the Internet...'

'Was I? Tea? I found the biscuits...'

'Sit and relax.' He moved towards the kitchen counter, threw a glance over his shoulder. 'How are things doing in your shop?'

'I beg your pardon?'

'You've been away...' he brought the pot of tea to the table along with the biscuits '... for longer than anticipated. Do you have reliable people working with you who can pick up the slack?'

He angled a chair so that he was sitting close to her, their knees almost touching, relaxing back with one arm slung over the back of the chair, the other resting on the table as he idly played with his mug.

'They're very good.' Celia cradled the mug with both hands. She was so alert to him sitting close to her that her nerves were all over the place as she tried to relax, telling him about her shop and what was going on in her absence while he listened in silence, head tilted to one side.

'You haven't stopped working while we've been here.' She adroitly changed the subject because his focus was so intense. 'Don't you trust the people who work with you?'

'They're good but when it comes to the crux, the only person I trust for the big stuff is myself.'

'Poor you if that means that you're condemned never to have time off,' she said lightly, eyes flicking to his serious, thoughtful face and just as quickly skittering away.

'But I'm not the only one with a few trust issues, am I?' Leandro murmured softly and Celia's eyes shot back to his face with alarm.

'I trust my colleagues one hundred per cent!'

'That's not what I'm talking about.'

'Then I don't know where you're going with this.' She jutted her chin at a defiant angle and her eyes widened in shock when he reached out and gently, absently and only for a few seconds touched the beating pulse at the base of her neck.

'Your body is telling a different story.'

He sat back while Celia stared at him, dumbfounded. Where his finger had rested was on fire. The heat started at that small spot and radiated all the way through her, sparking a fire inside her that made her want to leap out of the chair and dive right back into the freezing cold outside.

'Why are you so nervous when you're around me? No.' He held up one hand and half smiled. 'When I surprised you outside, you jumped a mile...'

'I wasn't expecting you! You should have been working——'

'And you're skittish around me...are you going to deny it? To me, that could only mean one of two things.'

'I don't want to have this conversation with you, Leandro. I...it's a pointless conversation and I don't like you...speculating about me.'

'Of course I'm going to speculate. We're here together, "cooped up" as you put it. Speculation is a by-product of the circumstances.'

'Not for me.'

'Liar.' He looked at her in silence just long enough for her to get the feeling that he was somehow seeing straight into her head, rummaging around and finding all those taboo thoughts that were whirling there.

Leandro noted every nuance of pink colour creeping into her cheeks. He registered the darkening of her eyes, the slight flare of her nostrils, and felt a surge of satisfaction that shocked him in its intensity.

How long had he had this urge to take her out of hiding? Had he even recognised his curiosity for what it was? Stronger than common sense? No, because he had never been this curious about anyone in his life before. What was it about her? Was it really just a case of curiosity being a natural by-product of their enforced isolation, as he had told her? He refused to contemplate the notion that somehow, without him realising it, she had managed to find a way to get under his skin. No woman was capable of doing that and many had tried over the years. He was inured against that and he liked it like that.

So this was...fun. More than that

'Either you're aware of me on a level that's not just about us being here together...' He waited for her to say something but she didn't. She didn't meet his eyes either and discomfort was written all over her face.

He was playing with fire. She wasn't his type. She was a woman who wanted a relationship, a proper, full-blown relationship with the end result of a ring on a finger and a walk up an aisle. He knew that he should steer clear of her. He might enjoy women, but he never set out to break hearts and he wasn't going to start now.

'Or maybe...' his voice was husky and just a little unsteady '...you have trust issues because someone hurt you in the past. Is that it?' But still he played with the tantalising thought that underneath the defensive exterior, she fancied him. It was pointless pretending that he didn't fancy her. From the start, there had been something about her that had pulled him in.

Skewered by those deep, dark eyes and prisoner of a line of questioning she knew could so easily unpick her fragile defences against him, Celia said hesitantly, 'I was engaged once.'

He was shocked. His reaction was so open and so extreme that she couldn't help but smile.

'People do get engaged, Leandro, and sometimes those engagements don't work out. You should know that more than anyone else.'

'They do,' Leandro murmured. 'What happened?'

* * *

Celia shrugged. She'd opened a door and now feelings that had been buried for a long time poured through her. She was rusty when it came to talking about it. The last time she *had* had been years ago, in the immediate aftermath, when there had been superficial explanations all round, to friends, to her family, squashing their concern even though she had been hurting inside, feeling like a gullible fool.

She expected to revisit those feelings now but instead she was surprised to find that she wasn't in the least bit sad at the memories of what had gone wrong for her and Martin. It was just something that had happened.

She began telling him, going round in circles and picking up threads of the past and interweaving them, feeling a weight lift from her shoulders.

'You're a good listener,' she finished, embarrassed at how much she had opened up.

'You sound surprised.'

'I wouldn't have expected it of you.'

'You still keep in touch with your ex?'

'On Facebook.' Celia shrugged. 'They post a lot of family shots.'

'Still have feelings for him?'

Celia laughed shortly. 'It may have taken

me a while to get over the hurt, but no, I don't have feelings for Martin, aside from friendship, which was really all there ever was.'

'Yet…he's still influencing how you live your life…'

'We're *all* influenced by our past,' Celia defended stoutly, then she paused and looked at him with speculation. 'Aren't you?'

Leandro flushed and then relaxed back with a lazy, charming smile. 'Absolutely. Are you hanging on to hear more?'

'Well, you *did* just hear my entire backstory.'

'So I did,' Leandro conceded. He hesitated, unfamiliar with anyone asking him about his private life. He was aware that his Keep Off signs were very good at doing their job, at making people know just what lines to stand behind. Yet it felt different sitting here far away from reality, locked up in a bubble with a green-eyed woman who teased his senses as no one ever had. Besides, where was the harm in sticking to the bare bones of his past? For the first time, it hit him that his well-ordered life, where he was the master of his universe and answerable to no one, also had its own hidden drawbacks. An ivory tower might protect against people getting in, but did it also prevent him, in the end, from getting out?

He dismissed that weird bout of introspection. It was no big deal. When they left, they would both return to their lives, two ships that briefly passed in the night. It wasn't as though they moved in remotely similar circles so the chances of them ever meeting again were minimal, unless it happened through Julie, but his friendship with his ex, should this break-up be permanent, would simply resume where it had left off. A one-on-one meeting every so often because of their shared past.

'My father,' Leandro mused thoughtfully, 'had no money. No, I tell a lie. He had a good life working on someone else's ranch, obeying someone else's orders, and the truth is he was happy with that. My mother left, and when she left she took his hopes and dreams with her.' Leandro's mouth thinned and his thoughts swirled around the words he hadn't said. The truth was that Leandro saw as weakness his father's acceptance of his lot, the way he had allowed the collapse of his marriage to tarnish the rest of his life. Too much given away. It would be something he, Leandro, would never allow.

'So when it comes to the past influencing the present? There you have it. I watched my father settle for less that he was worth and I decided that I would never do the same.' In danger of the atmosphere getting a little too serious for his liking, he lightened the mood with the ghost of a smile. 'So here I am. I'm at the top of the food chain and that's exactly where I want to be.'

'And your father?'

'Would you believe he's still living in the same house on the ranch even though I've told him a million times that I can buy him any-thing he wants, anywhere he wants?'

'Because your dreams aren't his.' Celia felt the intimacy of shared confidences wrap around her in a dangerous stranglehold and she stood up to begin tidying the mugs and biscuits.

She could feel his eyes boring into her. She wanted to ask him about his mother and she wondered whether he was even aware of how much he gave away by the bitterness in his voice when he mentioned her.

He was so deeply, bewitchingly complex and she shivered and slanted her eyes to glance at him, to find that he was staring at her, his expression broodingly intense.

'I should...go and get changed...' she murmured, backing away. She was doing it again…being skittish around him. What conclusions was he reaching? The one she dared not say out loud? That she fancied him? He was dangerous and she loathed the thought of danger so why was she so drawn to him?

'I'll see you later for dinner.' He vaulted upright, strolled towards the window and peered out at a landscape washed in grey and white, then he turned to her. 'With the weather like this and no Internet…we could be spending a lot more time together than we'd anticipated. I hope you don't mind…'

'Why should I?' Celia could hear the brittleness in her voice but she met his languid gaze steadily, challenging her body to let her down. 'The walking is lovely provided you wrap up well, and for me? I'm not reliant on the Internet. I brought my computer for sketching and I can do that anywhere…'

CHAPTER FIVE

CELIA TOOK HER time with a bath. She had a couple of hours to kill before heading right back down to the kitchen and she intended to kill them on her own, getting her thoughts in order so that when she faced Leandro later on, she would be in control.

She dreaded the thought of him wandering the house like a lost soul without his Internet connection to the rest of the world. They had shared something back there in the kitchen and, whatever it was, it had wreaked havoc with her composure.

It was a little after six by the time she made it down to a silent kitchen. There was no Leandro waiting to send her nervous system into freefall, and for an hour or so Celia enjoyed the peace, even though she had one ear out for his footsteps and an eye on the kitchen door for when he pushed it open.

She was puzzled when, at a little before

seven, there was still no sign of him. He usually enjoyed the relaxation of cooking but now, fancying that he had maybe become wrapped up in something work-related that didn't require an Internet connection, she began preparing some dinner for them both.

She switched the radio on. It was the one old-fashioned gadget in the uber-modern kitchen and she hummed along to old tunes as she tackled the larder, pulling out rice and beans and some tuna and wondering how creative she could get with the ingredients.

It was only when the eight o'clock news came on that it dawned on her that Leandro wasn't going to show up.

Bitter disappointment swamped any feelings of relief that she wouldn't have to face him.

She *wanted* to see him, wanted to feel the fizz of excitement coursing through her. Why pretend that he didn't excite her? He did.

But maybe he had had time to regret the fact that they had bridged a gap. Maybe he had stopped to think that encouraging anything with her would be stupid because, as he had told her from the beginning, she wasn't his type. He didn't go for the romantic sort. Had he got a little spooked at the idea that she might start getting feelings for him?

Celia burned with embarrassment when she thought about that but what if it was true?

Deflated, she made the most of the meal she cooked. Relaxing on her own no longer seemed to have any appeal. She headed up to her suite, slowing her steps as she passed his bedroom. She didn't want to knock but the impulse was so strong. She *had* to find out for herself whether he was avoiding her for all the wrong reasons. She was in *no danger* of letting her guard slip around him! She had no idea how she could manoeuvre the conversation in a direction whereby she could make that perfectly clear but somehow it felt vital that she do so.

Her hand hovering in front of the door, her mouth dry, the decision was taken out of her hands when she heard a crash and then she didn't bother to knock at all.

Celia pushed the door open and stepped into a darkened room. She had to blink for her eyes to adjust.

Leandro was in the process of pulling himself up onto the bed and, without thinking, she raced towards him, heart beating a mile a minute.

'What's wrong?' she asked.

There was panic in her voice. She circled his waist with her arm, helping him up and then straightening the bedside table, which had crashed to the ground under the impact of his weight.

The feel of him, his skin against hers, burnt into her as she leapt back to look at him with mounting alarm.

He had flopped back onto the bed, half propping himself up on the pillows. He loosely draped a dark-coloured duvet over his body but, save for a pair of boxers, he was completely naked and while she did her utmost not to look, she couldn't help herself.

He was all shadows and angles and absolutely, stunningly beautiful. In repose, he was a work of art, broad-shouldered, lean-hipped, a vision of beauty and strength.

She hovered by the side of the bed and flinched when he switched on the lamp, which she had repositioned on the bedside table.

'I feel like crap,' he rasped hoarsely, opening one baleful eye.

'When? How? You were fine earlier…'

'Got up here, had a shower, had a sudden urge to climb into bed and fell asleep.' He groaned. 'Woke up with a splitting headache, started getting out of bed and that's when you heard me. I reached for the table but ended up toppling it over.'

'You're burning up.' Hand on his forehead, Celia went from being agonisingly *aware* of him to briskly recognising that she had a patient on her hands who would need taking care of.

The distinction was a blessing. She could deal with being Florence Nightingale. It was a lot less stressful than trying to work out how she could convince him whatever effect he had on her was all in his mind!

'Do you have a first-aid kit?'

'Bathroom.'

'Take these.' This when she had returned with some water in a glass she had found on one of the inset shelves by the huge, swimming-pool-sized bath.

'I don't do tablets.'

'In that case—' she rested the tablets on the table, stood back and folded her arms '—you can do a raging fever and aches and pains instead. Your choice.'

Leandro held out his hand and she duly put the tablets into it and watched as he swallowed them before settling back down, eyes closed.

'Are you hungry? Would you like something to eat?'

The question hung in the air but by the time she reached the door, he was asleep.

Leandro slept fitfully for the next couple of hours. Celia checked in on him and when, at a little before midnight, his fever began climbing once again, she repeated her tablet routine although, this time, he didn't argue.

This time, when their eyes met in the darkened room, his were alert whatever the state of his aching body.

He swallowed the tabs but when she turned to leave, he stayed her, his fingers circling her wrist, tugging her gently back so that she half stumbled onto the bed.

'I should thank you for this,' he rasped and Celia, hyper conscious of his fingers on her wrist and the pad of his thumb idly gently stroking the tender sensitive skin, muttered something and nothing.

Celia licked her lips and tried a reassuring smile on for size but those small, stroking movements...

They were flooding her treacherous body with heat. She wanted him to stop, wanted to yank her hand away and rub where he'd touched but she didn't because she was enjoying it too much. She was, oh, so tempted to touch him back and the strength of that temptation terrified her because it was so new.

'For what?' She laughed jerkily. 'All I've done is bring you some tablets and water and checked in occasionally to make sure you haven't...worsened...'

'It's after midnight.'

'I know.'

'You must be tired and yet you've still checked in…'

'Leandro, has no one ever taken care of you before? I mean,' she added softly, quickly, 'when you've been laid up? It's no big deal. My brother's older than me but we both live in London and, honestly, as soon as he sneezes twice, he calls me and begs me to come over and look after him.'

'I thought he was a free spirit.' There was a smile in Leandro's voice.

This felt so good, so relaxed, their voices low murmurs in the bedroom and the curtains letting in just a slither of silvery light here and there.

'He's as free as a bird until he gets a cold.' She smiled back.

'You're very close, aren't you?'

'Yes. We are. Small village close to a small town where kids still play outside without supervision and mostly everyone knows everyone else. We went to the same school and, even though he's older, his friends all somehow seemed to know my friends because they were related or neighbours…so yes…'

'That's why you drifted into an engagement that wasn't right…'

Celia shrugged. She'd already told him about Martin so what was the point in being coy on the subject if he chose to raise it again? She'd opened a door and she didn't regret it because it had felt like a release.

'Like I said…'

'You didn't tell your brother how much it affected you?'

'I suppose I was embarrassed…ashamed that I'd been so naïve.' She looked away and then confessed, in a low voice, 'And Martin found someone else so fast, someone tall and athletic and pretty and really nice as well…'

Leandro heard the vulnerability in her voice and his heart clenched.

It was one thing to admit to a broken engagement, which she had. She could tell him why it had ended, a simple youthful error of judgement, not that uncommon in the great scheme of things. But now, he could detect the place where it had really hurt and it felt like something twisting inside him.

She had lost confidence in her own sexuality because the guy she'd mistakenly thought she'd end up with had found someone else in record time and someone else who was probably, physically, the polar opposite of her.

He reached out to push her hair back and

then let his hand linger, tangled in her hair. He felt her breathe in sharply and saw the widening of her eyes but she wasn't pulling away.

She was still in a jumper and her jogging bottoms, hadn't changed into whatever it was she slept in. He wondered what it was she did sleep in. In that suite of rooms so close to his.

'You're still lucky,' he murmured, sliding his finger across her cheek, which was as smooth as satin. 'You have a support system that's been there for you through thick and thin.'

'And you haven't.' Celia was just stating a fact.

'No. Which—' there was wry amusement in his voice '—is probably why I have never fallen ill. I've always known that I wouldn't have anyone around to play nursemaid and mop my fevered brow.'

Celia thought that there would be a long line of women all dying to play nursemaid to Leandro. She figured that he would have to erect a wall of steel to stop them from stampeding into his house, bearing thermometers and cups of tea, able and willing to minister to his every need.

She didn't have to join too many dots to figure out what he wasn't saying.

Leandro didn't *want* anyone to play nursemaid with him. He didn't *want* that level of involvement from any woman because that would have encouraged a conversation about *commitment* that he would never have.

She was here now and what choice did he have when it came to nursemaids?

She was the sole candidate and so she knew that she shouldn't be reading anything into the intimacy swirling around them now.

Logic having asserted itself, Celia knew that she should drily tell him exactly what she was thinking, then she should change the subject and leave because he needed to get some sleep and so did she, but instead she remained silent.

Her body was melting. It was on fire and, deep inside, the bloom of a craving she had never felt before was spreading through her. It made her limbs feel heavy and, between her legs, warm wetness was pooling, liquid heat that made her breathing sluggish.

The dangerous notion that somehow the here and now was *real* threaded a way through common sense and cold reason. After all, hadn't they confided in one another? With the snow falling outside, thick and dense and wrapping them in a bubble? She felt that he'd opened up to her in ways he hadn't foreseen and she'd certainly done the same, telling him about Martin and about how she'd felt when he'd settled down with someone else five minutes after she'd returned his engagement ring. Beautiful, leggy, *nice* Annabelle.

She leant into him and closed her eyes to the kiss she knew was coming, one she wanted so much. The kiss that would clear her head of everything, take her back to a time before disappointment and disillusionment had made their mark. And yet, as his lips met hers, she was still rocked to the very core.

Her hands feverishly smoothed his broad, hard chest, with its sprinkling of dark hair. She didn't even want to come up for air! Who needed to breathe?

As his mouth travelled along her neck, she gasped and sifted her fingers through his dark hair, pulling him towards her.

Her breasts felt heavy and sensitive. She wasn't wearing a bra but under the layers, the thermal vest and the jumper, she could feel the scrape of her nipples against the fabric.

She longed to lose herself completely in the present but, of course, that was not how she had been brought up. She'd been brought up to think about consequences. She pushed him back, but it was like surfacing from a warm, cosy blanket to the bitter cold of Arctic air.

He released her instantly, but when he pulled back she could see that his breathing was as uneven as hers.

'Leandro,' she husked. 'That… I'm sorry…'

'Not your fault.'

'That shouldn't have happened.' She was almost disappointed when, after a moment's hesitation, he raked his fingers through his hair and muttered agreement.

'I… I don't know what…' She laughed self-consciously.

'I would never make a pass at a woman before knowing that there's an invite on the table…the kind of guy who touches what's out of bounds…' Leo said.

Celia thought that the last thing she had been a few moments ago was *out of bounds*. She'd matched his kiss with equal passion, as though the walls of the dam had dropped away and nothing could stop the torrent of uncontrolled water.

'I'll go now…get some sleep.'

'Yes.' Their eyes met. His kiss was still on his mouth and she wanted more.

So she was the romantic type. She would always be the romantic type, a woman who would never allow lessons learnt to warp her vision of *True Love*. He didn't get it, himself, but then no two people were ever the same.

That said…she'd closed herself off from men since she'd returned that engagement ring to the guy who'd promptly replaced her with someone else. That said…whatever fairy tales she believed in when it came to Love, she was too scared to seek it out because of what had happened. He'd seen those shadows on her face when she'd told him about her replacement, and he'd known there and then that the depth of her hurt had come not just from the bruising of her ego because her engagement had ended in tears. *That* was something that would have shaken her, but its effect wouldn't have been lasting. He'd believed her when she'd said that she'd understood how right the ex had been in calling it off. Too young…invisible pressure to drift into something everyone expected…in love with the feeling of being in love.

But then her ex had hooked up with another woman no sooner than he'd finished his *Dear John* or, in this case, *Dear Jill* speech to her. And not just that…he'd hooked up with a woman Celia felt was superior to her physically. Leandro was sure that she couldn't have been further from the truth on that count, but the fact remained that self-confidence in herself as a *woman* had taken a beating and *that* was what had held her back.

She fancied him. Leandro had felt it in the urgency of her mouth against his and the eager caressing of her hands and, hell, he couldn't remember fancying any woman as much as he did her.

But, in her head, sex was all tied up with Love and how wrong she was.

What she needed was to get her self-confidence back, to know that she was a beautiful, vital woman who could pick and choose from whatever pond she decided to throw her rod into.

Without self-confidence, she would remain hiding in the shadows for ever, waiting for someone to come along and tick all the boxes, without her having to do any hard work to get there.

'Or...' Leandro let that one word drop into the silence and linger there for a few seconds '...you could sleep here.'

His dark eyes challenged hers.

'Let's not pretend... We want one another. A lot.'

'That's not the point,' Celia stammered.

'Isn't it?'

* * *

Celia heard the warm persuasion in his voice and shivered. 'You can't just do as you please in life.'

'Why not?'

'Because…' Her voice petered out. She was rooted to the spot but when he patted the space on the bed that she had seconds before vacated, she felt her trembling legs take a hesitant step towards him, then two steps, then she was perched on the side.

'Because you're scared,' Leandro said gently. 'You're scared you're going to be hurt if you allow yourself to just let go.'

'I…' She shook her head in confusion.

'You've spent years holding back from involvement because you lost your self-confidence when the guy you thought had your back disappeared with another woman in the blink of an eye.'

'Maybe.' She looked at him with angry defiance, but his voice was thoughtful and soft and her anger was skin deep. She'd never had a conversation like this with anyone and it made her feel raw and vulnerable, but he was right, wasn't he?

'You won't be hurt with me,' Leandro told her quietly. 'I'm not your type, remember?'

'No. You're not…'

'We're two adults who fancy one another and, of course, I will completely respect whatever decision you make, so if you choose to walk through that door right now and not look back, then you can trust me that I'll back off straight away. I checked the snow earlier on the way to the bathroom and it's clearing. We will be out of here soon enough and you can pretend that none of this ever happened.'

'You won't be hurt with me...'

But, Celia thought, would she hurt herself if she walked away? Would she regret for ever this chance to have just the sort of adventure that might do her so much good in the long run? They weren't emotionally involved... she could touch without fear...she could let herself feel and be a woman again.

She reached out with one trembling hand and cupped the side of his face and then moaned softly when he turned her palm over and kissed it, his dark eyes still on her.

'I want you,' she sighed in surrender and Leandro pulled her against him and buried his head into her neck, tugging her jumper so that he could nuzzle her shoulder.

'But...' she added.

'But...?'

'But are you feeling okay for...?'

Leandro loosed a low, sexy laugh. 'I think the best thing is exercise...'

Half lying on him, Celia laughed and then smiled and hoisted herself into an upright position, eager to get her clothes off but too shy to actually do it.

Leandro sensed her hesitation and understood it. He slipped his hand under the cotton jumper and gently smoothed her shoulder and with each languid motion, the top was pushed further down her arm until, with impatience, she did as he'd hoped and pulled it off with abandonment.

He'd dreamt of a feast and was faced with a banquet, such was the stunning sexiness of her curves. Full breasts pushed against a cotton vest. No bra. He could just about make out the stiff protrusion of her nipples and the sight made him feel faint with desire.

He wanted to tear the vest off and cup those luscious breasts. He wanted to touch and taste and then touch again and keep touching until he knew every succulent inch of a body that was designed to drive a red-blooded man mad.

But he was going to take it slowly. She'd roused something protective in him. It surprised him but he wasn't going to fight it.

Something about being in this cold, silent place, as close to the wilderness as he had ever been, was playing games with his common sense and he was enjoying the unexpected journey.

He angled her so that she was astride him. He was sitting up and here, in this position, they were eye to eye, their bodies so close he could feel the heat from hers and her warm breath softly against his face. So close he could pull her towards him and kiss her senseless, which was what he was aching to do. His erection was so steel hard that it was painful and he had to shift a little to relieve the discomfort.

When she tried to snuggle against him, like a little mole seeking the safety of its burrow, he gently eased her back and smiled.

'You're nervous.'

'A little,' Celia admitted breathlessly. 'It's been a while…'

'You're beautiful.'

Celia laughed self-consciously and blushed.

'Whatever feelings you've had about your ex…' Leandro sifted his fingers through her hair and left them there to gently caress and then cup her cheek '…forget about thinking that somehow it had anything to do with how

you look, because you're the sexiest woman
I've ever shared my bed with.'

'You want to put me at ease...'

'I never lie.' His voice was low and husky
as he trailed one finger down the deep in-
dent of her cleavage and then over the vest
to circle her protuberant nipples, zeroing in
on the stiffened buds and grazing the pads
of his thumbs over them. She groaned softly
and arched towards him, head flung back and
her eyes fluttering shut as sensation replaced
thought. 'Although, it's true, I *do* want to put
you at ease.'

She was already at ease.

So relaxed that she quivered with longing
when he pulled the thermal up and over her
breasts, freeing them to the pinch of cool air.

He straightened, manoeuvring them both
into a position where her breasts hung heavy
and ripe, close enough to almost brush his
chest.

He weighed them in his hands and had to
close his eyes and breathe deeply just to control himself. He'd never been premature in
his responses with any woman, but he was
facing a challenge now. Even more of a challenge when he finally looked at her flushed
face and her parted mouth and inhaled the
scent of pure lust.

With a stifled growl, he replaced his fingers with his mouth. She had larger than average nipples, each pink disc topped with the stiffened bud against which he rolled his tongue, licking and tasting and tugging until she was whimpering and rocking on him.

How had she managed to find just where to move, rubbing his erection in the sort of way that was sending his body into a slow orbit?

He couldn't keep up the slow tempo any longer. Not if he wanted to emerge with his masculine pride intact.

What remained of their clothes came off in a hurry.

Boxers...vest...underwear...jogging bottoms...all hit the floor at speed. Her nakedness against his, her soft, rounded curves were driving him crazy. And had he really been laid up? Feverish? He couldn't remember. The only fever he felt now was the searing heat of uncontrollable craving.

She was still straddling him. He eased her off. He was desperate to do more than have her rotate her sexy hips and get him so steamed up he wanted to explode.

He nuzzled the soft underside of her breasts while his hand travelled down to cup her between her legs. He pressed gently, felt her wetness and kept just the right amount of pressure there to remind her of the pleasure coming her way.

He didn't have to guide her hand to him. She was exploring him with impatience, curving her body to his and opening her legs to accommodate his hand.

She stroked his spine and then feathered tiny circles at the base and then ran her hand along his waist and everywhere she touched lit him up like a match hitting dry tinder.

When she circled the thick shaft of his penis, he groaned and fell back for a few seconds.

With very little effort, she could take him right over the edge the way those hands and fingers were working and, however novel and enjoyable the prospect was, he had other ideas in his head for where this was going.

With a low laugh, he flipped her and slowly, with devastating intent, he made his way down her body, touching and feeling and moistening with the flick of his tongue.

She responded without inhibition. Whatever shyness she'd felt at the start, when she'd stared down at him with those big green, innocent eyes, had evaporated like dew in the summer sun and every touch elicited a whimper of pleasure.

Leandro kissed, suckled, nuzzled. He circled her belly button with his tongue. He stroked under her arms, along her arms and licked her fingers one by one.

He let his hand drift along her inner thigh and allowed his knuckles to brush against the soft folds of her womanhood in a way that teased and aroused, and only when she demanded more did he dip his fingers in to feel the wet heat of her arousal.

He felt that it had been a long time coming…this…this feeling of wanting to lose himself in someone else.

Physically, of course.

Always just *physically* but even so…it was joyous.

Their bodies were on fire when, at last, he fumbled his way to retrieve a condom from his wallet and entered her. Her slippery wetness welcomed his hardness, wrapped like honeyed sweetness around his shaft and he was alive to her every moan of intense satisfaction as he thrust long and deep into her.

They came quicker than he wanted, but even as his body stiffened and arched and he felt the exquisite shudder of release he was acknowledging that he didn't want this to be the first and last of their couplings.

He held her close.

'Stay.'

* * *

Celia, basking in the warm glow of absolute fulfilment, her mind hazy with every pleasure chemical her body had released during an orgasm that had left her weak, swivelled so that she was half draped over him, her arm resting on his chest and her chin propped in the crook of her elbow.

'Huh?'

'Stay. Here. In bed with me. All day and all night.'

Celia laughed but a little bubble of pleasure swelled inside her because his dark eyes were deadly serious even though there was just a ghost of a smile on his lips.

Alarm bells rang in her head. Spend all day and all night with him? Share his bed? For how long? And what happened next in that scenario?

But her heart was safe. This was sex and she'd flung herself headlong into it because, by gosh, it had been a while. *For ever.* To be touched, for her body to be alive again after years buried in deep ice…it had felt *good*, better than *good*.

Leandro had opened a door for her to re-enter the living, breathing, vital world she had left behind.

'I hear the sound of a guy who can't spend

all day working…' she teased, but her voice was a little breathless.

'You hear the sound of a guy who's never had such good sex in his life. It's the sound of a guy who wants more. Do you? Want more? Of this?' To emphasise his point, he stroked the curve of her waist and let his hand rest there.

'While we're here…' Celia let that hang in the air between them, willing him to pick up the baton and run with it, to paint a bigger picture than something that would last until the snow melted, but he didn't.

He said in a soft, sexy purr, while he feathered the soft down between her thighs, 'While we're here. The snow's falling and we're locked away here until…who knows when? Even when it stops, it'll be at least a day or so until I can get the helicopter in a fit state to take to the skies. And in the meantime…'

'In the meantime, we enjoy…this…'

'We're on the same page, Celia.' Leandro sifted his fingers through the tangled copper curls that fanned over her face and shoulders in riotous disarray. He traced the outline of her mouth with his finger. 'This is fun. I figure we could both do with a little of that. A little no-strings-attached fun.' He sighed and

for a few moments, he fell back to stare at the
ceiling and then he held her close against him
and said, face averted, 'I thought I had my
life sorted when Julie and I got engaged.' He
turned to her but still held her close to him.
'You don't get it, but it was an arrangement
that worked for me. I can't love and this offered friendship without the complications of
anything more, while helping her father, repaying a debt. Yes, we would have had, what
you might call, an open marriage, but a very,
very discreet one.'

'You're so cynical, Leandro.'

'I'm realistic. I have no desire for children,
but companionship? Maybe so...'

'So you have uncomplicated fun here, with
me...'

'And then return to whatever awaits on the
personal front. Charles, at least, is sorted as
far as his finances go. The rest he will have to
come to terms with. And you, my darling...'
he smiled a little more '...you get to let go
of whatever demons you've had and return
to London refreshed. The perfect guy awaits
you out there. Maybe you won't be afraid to
take up the challenge of trying to find him.'

Celia thought that that felt about right.
Didn't it? He should have sounded arrogant
in assuming that this brief sojourn was some-

how doing her the favour of setting her on the right path of finding true love, that, thanks to him, she was now freed from her demons. He didn't. He sounded sincere and she was confused because she wasn't sure whether she liked that or not.

But of course she did, she told herself stoutly.

And she sure as heck still wanted this man. Fiercely and passionately and for as long as she could have him. She curled against him and smiled back, at peace with her decision.

'Yes, Leandro. While the snow falls…'

CHAPTER SIX

'*There's a Celia Drew to see you.*'

It was not a call Leandro had expected to take three weeks after he returned to London.

He sat back in his swivel chair, surprising his PA by telling her to send up his unexpected visitor and to cancel his morning meetings until he told her otherwise.

He vaulted out of his chair and strolled to the bank of windows overlooking the dank, crowded streets several stories below. So, she'd had second thoughts. Maybe she had revisited his offer and decided that taking him up on it might not be such a bad idea after all. He perversely hoped so because he would then be able to tell her that it was now off the table.

Which it most decidedly was.

Leandro's lips thinned at the unsavoury recollection of how their stint in Scotland had concluded.

A week living in a bubble. It had felt as though he had found himself inside one of those snow globes—shaken it and watched the white swirl of snowflakes covering everything for a few breathless, magical seconds.

He had gone to get a job done and had persuaded her to come because he'd needed her there. His objective had been simple—confront his runaway ex-fiancée, fill her in on what was happening with her father, remind her of the agreement they had reached to safeguard his financial future in a way that would salvage his pride, and to check out for himself what was going on with her mysterious lover who had bounced along and screwed everything up.

Simple.

Unfortunately, there had been no runaway ex-fiancée to confront and, instead, he had found himself trapped in his snow globe with a woman who had utterly bewitched him. For the first time in his life, well-laid plans had veered off-piste at dizzying speed.

Just thinking about it now made his teeth snap together with impatience and frustration.

He should have known that the temptation to touch would have been too much. He should have known because he'd sensed something intensely, sexually compelling about her from the very first minute he had clapped eyes on her.

She broke all the rules when it came to the sort of woman he tended to go out with. She had appealed to him on some weird level he hadn't quite been able to understand and, maybe the second he'd clocked their isolation, he'd known that lurking in the safety of his office would not have been enough to kill off his very inconvenient attraction.

He'd wanted her and she'd wanted him and somehow he'd let her get under his skin.

The sex had been mind-blowing.

He'd stepped out of time, forgotten the rules and regulations that governed his uber-controlled life. Why? How had that happened? How had the walls he had constructed with such painstaking care been so easy to breach? And why on earth now did it feel so liberating?

Liberating enough for him to lose sight of the fact that what had happened between them had been a moment in time.

He had offered her more. When that snow had melted and the helicopter had signalled the return of normality, instead of shaking hands and saying *Goodbye…it's been nice…*

look me up if you're ever in the area... he'd
asked her to carry on.

'*This isn't over yet,*' he'd husked, basking
in the warm glow of post-coital satisfaction
and knowing that she was as well. '*Why call
it a day when we're still hot for one another?*'

It hadn't crossed his mind that she would
turn him down. Why would it have? She'd
known the enticing benefits that came with
dating him. He hadn't needed to spell them
out and front-row tickets to a fashion show
had been just the tip of the iceberg.

And if she wasn't interested in weekends
at Lake Como or prime seats at the theatre
or eating in the finest restaurants that money
could buy? No problem. He would happily
have ditched the lot, closed the front door and
whiled away the hours between the sheets.

Still, it hadn't troubled him when she'd
very politely but very firmly thanked him
for the kind offer and declined.

Now she was here.

Had she had second thoughts?

He wouldn't blame her. She'd taken him up
on the tickets to the fashion show. He knew
that because he'd checked. Had that opened
her eyes to what she might enjoy if she had a
change of heart about his offer?

Or maybe she'd just realised that she still

wanted him, plain and simple. Maybe she'd spent the past three weeks tossing and turning at night in bed, thinking about him and wishing that they were tossing and turning together.

It was galling for Leandro to think that he had laughed, shrugged...*you win a few, you lose a few*...and accepted rejection with nonchalance because, face it, there were plenty of other fish in the sea, only to find that she was still in his head three weeks later.

Leandro didn't know how that computed but now that she was here, now that she had shown up out of the blue, he was feeling good for the first time since he'd locked the front door of his place in Scotland.

He was ready, waiting and half smiling as his dividing door was pushed open, as she was announced by his PA, at which point he spun round on his heel and headed back to the chair behind his impressive mahogany desk.

Celia, having weathered the worst week of her life, had been gripped by a sense of inevitability as she had stood, hovering and indecisive, in front of the towering glass spire in which Leandro's offices were housed.

It had taken every scrap of moral fibre not to turn tail and flee.

Unfortunately, there was no choice in the matter. This was going to be step one of a journey she had not anticipated and the prospect of all the other steps to follow made her feel sick.

She'd wondered whether he would even agree to see her at all and had worked out what she would do in that eventuality.

The bald fact of the matter was she had turned down his suggestion that they carry on seeing one another when they were back in London. Until such time as it came to a natural conclusion. He hadn't had to say that in so many words, but the implication had hung in the air between them like the sword of Damocles.

So much tantalising promise, dangling in front of her eyes like a banquet in a famine and, oh, how she had longed to jump at his offer. How she'd yearned to keep the door firmly shut against reality and continue to live in the delicious bubble they had constructed for themselves.

She had been deep frozen and he had brought her to life. That was how it had felt out there in the middle of nowhere, with the snow locking them in and making it easy to pretend that what they had was real.

It wasn't. Not for him. It was real for *her*. She'd gone into a situation with her eyes wide open and yet had been totally unprepared for the consequences.

Again!

She'd cheerfully told herself that he wasn't her type, at least not on any level that counted for anything. Yes, he was utter physical perfection and, sure, she reacted to him as any woman would, but there was no way sleeping with him could get complicated. Complicated was when emotions entered the equation and she was older and wiser and well able to recognise the sort of guy who could introduce complications.

But he'd touched her and she'd melted and he'd kept on touching and holding and captivating her and, bit by bit, the ground had shifted under her feet without her even realising.

She'd gone from hostile and suspicious to enthralled in supersonic speed and when the snow had finally petered out and London had beckoned, she'd been horrified to realise just how hard she had fallen for him.

Not just *fallen*. Fallen somehow implied she could pick herself up and dust herself down as she had with Martin, even though at the time she hadn't realised just how easy that had been. She'd been too busy feeling sorry for herself and humiliated because he had found her replacement in record time.

No, she had lost herself in Leandro and she'd known that finding her way back from that place was going to take strength she wasn't even sure she had.

And the only way she could even begin to do that was to walk away from him.

He hadn't even bothered to hide the fact that, as far as he was concerned, whatever they had wasn't going to last. It would run its course and come to an end, probably when he got bored with the novelty of having her around.

At which point, he would pick it back up with the sort of women he was really drawn to.

But fate had had other ideas.

It had been bad enough dithering outside the impressive building, but it had been ten times worse when she'd stood in front of that granite counter, with the bustle of city professionals swarming around her, and been told that, yes, Leandro would see her.

'Hadn't expected to see you.'

Leandro's dark, sexy drawl snapped her back to the present and Celia blinked as the door behind her gently clicked shut.

She'd barely paid any attention to her surroundings as she'd been shown up to his office and she hardly noticed them now. She was one hundred per cent riveted to Leandro's face, to the lazy sprawl of his big body

behind the desk and the uncanny way he had
of looking at her as though he could see right
down to her very soul.

How could she have forgotten just how
powerful his presence was? How shockingly
good-looking he was? Darker, harsher, more
forbidding than she remembered, but then
they were no longer in the same place, where
they were relaxed and laughing and all over
one another, eager to get back in the bed as
soon as they were out of it. Sometimes, not
even making it to the bedroom. He was back
to the guy she'd first met when he'd shown
up unannounced at her shop.

'I hope I'm not disturbing you.' Celia hadn't
moved one inch from the spot to which she
was rooted by the closed door. 'I thought I'd
try and catch you before you left.'

'What are you doing here? Just passing by?
Thought you'd swing by for old times' sake?'

Leandro had thought, when they'd parted
company, that the snowbound isolation of
their situation might have exaggerated her
sexual appeal, but the second she'd walked
into his office he'd known just how far off
target he'd been in that assumption.

He was grimly aware that his libido, which
had done less than zero on the two occasions

he had opted for distraction tactics and got in touch with a couple of women he knew, was now hale and hearty and ready to party.

He shifted uncomfortably in his chair and scowled.

'Sit.' He nodded to the chair positioned in front of his desk and couldn't help the fall of his gaze on her breasts, swaying under the… whatever it was she was wearing. What was she wearing? Some kind of suit and a jacket and some furry ankle boots.

She was nervous as hell, that much he could see, and it occurred to him that if she'd come to fling herself in his arms, then she surely wasn't dressed for the occasion. Not, he thought with a kick of masculine appreciation, that she didn't look as cute as hell in her get-up. Her hair was clipped back but, with almost no leap of his imagination, he could picture it as he had seen it so many times, in wild, copper disarray around her face.

Leandro breathed in deeply and half closed his eyes and fought against a bombardment of powerful, graphic images.

Watching him, stomach twisted with nervous tension, Celia couldn't help but notice just how unwelcoming he was. How fast he'd gone from the guy who'd gruffly but sincerely asked her to carry on what they had because he still wanted her to someone who was clearly put out that she'd shown up unexpectedly at his workplace. It hadn't occurred to her, but now she wondered whether he'd met someone else.

She walked to the chair on wobbly legs and fell into it but then she quickly gathered herself and looked at him.

'You're wondering what I'm doing here.'

'Is it to do with Julie? Your brother? I'm guessing not because everything seems to be roses and sunshine on that front.'

'Yes.' Celia grasped the lifeline of innocuous conversation because it gave her time for her nerves to steady. 'I don't know how Julie's father feels about it because I haven't spoken to her face to face yet, but I know Dan's over the moon and so are Mum and Dad.'

'So…if you're not here to discuss family matters, then why exactly are you here?'

Her silence, Leandro thought, was telling. He wanted her still so badly that it *hurt* and that, as much as anything else, enraged him because it signified just the sort of weakness he had spent a lifetime protecting himself against. A simple request, nothing more, and yet it felt like a stake of trust being driven into the ground, a vulnerability with someone else of the sort that should never happen. Had never happened.

His eyes cooled and his expression hardened.

'If you've come,' he inserted quietly into the awkward, lengthening silence, 'because you've decided that you want to pick up where we left off, after all, then I'm sorry to say that that window has closed.'

Uttering those words didn't give Leandro the satisfaction he'd expected but there was no way he had any intention of taking them back. He was, however, bemused by the expression on her face, which went from puzzled to incredulous to downright angry. Colour flared in her cheeks and she half rose from her chair only to abruptly sit back down.

'Believe it or not, that's *not* why I've come to see you, Leandro!'

'Then why?' Leandro asked.

'I'm beginning to wonder that myself,' Celia said in a driven undertone. 'I wouldn't have bothered you if I'd had a choice. I know that I turned you down and I know I probably...offended you...'

Leandro laughed with incredulity.

'Offended me? How? I thought we might have had a few more weeks of fun but the fact that you weren't interested in that option hardly tore my life to ribbons!'

Hearing that hurt and Celia felt the sting of tears push behind her eyelids.

'I'm here to tell you that I'm pregnant, Leandro.'

It still sounded surreal to her own ears. It would. Bearing in mind she hadn't said a word to anyone. It was something she was still holding to herself and coming to terms with as her whole world was turned upside down.

She'd barely been aware that her period was overdue until she developed an aversion to her usual morning cup of coffee and then, just like that, it hit her that her body was behaving differently and it wasn't just the coffee aversion. Her breasts had started feeling weird and she'd almost nodded off a couple of times when she'd been doing some sketching for a commission.

She'd known, *deep down*, but it had still come as a shock when that little stick had confirmed her worst fears.

She'd scrabbled around in her head trying to work out the when and the how, but everything had become a blur and the only thing that had become clear during those horrendous few days when she'd walked around in a daze was that she had to tell Leandro.

They might not have anything left between them but a handful of memories, and he might very well slam the door in her face when she broke the news, but she *had* to tell him because that was the person she was.

'You can't be.'

'I'm sorry.' Her eyes slid away from his ashen face to the window behind him. 'I know this is the last thing you want to hear but I had to come and tell you. I haven't come here to ask anything of you, just in case that's what you're thinking. I know what we had…er… ended a couple of weeks ago but I didn't think it would have been fair on you if I hadn't… filled you in. Well, you would have probably found out anyway, because of your connection with Julie…'

'How? How did this happen?' He waved one hand and then rubbed his eyes with his fingers and for a few seconds he said nothing at all, then he looked at her. 'No need to answer that. We…had a lot of fun and sometimes it's possible that I wasn't as careful as I might have been.' He sat back and briefly closed his eyes. 'Are you sure?'

'I did more than one test, Leandro. Of course, I'm more than happy to do a few more, but there's no doubt that I'm having a baby.' But his willingness to accept at least some of the responsibility was a weight off her shoulders.

All the attendant problems now crowded in on her and she blinked, suddenly vulnerable under the onslaught.

Before she could react, he had swerved around the desk and positioned himself next to her, half stooping so that they were on eye level.

'This isn't the right place to be having a conversation about this.' He raked his fingers through his hair but didn't take his eyes off her face.

'It's a shock, I know.' She began standing. Her legs were still wobbly but it was a relief now that she had said her piece. 'I'll leave you to mull things over.'

'What?' Leandro said sharply. *Mull things over?'*

'Yes. We can always talk again soon.'

'No, no, no. I think you've got the wrong end of the stick here, Celia. There's nothing to *mull over* that's going to propel me into reaching any kind of alternative conclusion. You're pregnant and it's my fault.'

'It takes two to tango.'

'We need privacy for this conversation.' He

was already moving towards a concealed door, pushing it so that it sprang open and reaching for a tan coat in the softest of cashmere.

'Where are we going?'

'My place.'

'What? No!'

'Why not?' Leandro strolled in front of her, invading her space for a couple of seconds, hands shoved deep in the pockets of the coat. His dark eyes ensnared her and the silence stretched taut.

Leandro's eyes drifted down, remorselessly drawn to her stomach, and it hit him hard that this was more than just a theoretical discussion about what happened when faced with an unexpected pregnancy.

She was carrying his child.

He felt shaken to his very foundations. Nothing in life had braced him for this eventuality. How had he ended up being cavalier, at least on one occasion he could remember when the distance from kitchen to bedroom to get protection had been a little too far, and not foreseen the consequences?

And yet now, as he stared down at her, what should have horrified him, didn't.

What should have filled him with resentment, didn't. He didn't feel the walls closing in. He felt…a surge of protectiveness that knocked him for six.

Where did *that* come from?

He'd never factored children into his life. Why would he? He'd seen the damage parents could do, he'd lived the unspoken sorrow born of growing up with the whiff of abandonment because, although he'd had his father, what child would not be affected by a mother who left him when he was barely out of nappies?

So having kids? Never been on the horizon. Easier to shelve that whole issue than take the risk of being an unwitting cause of hurt to a kid who hadn't asked to be born. He worked all the hours under the sun. That, for starters, augured badly for the sort of family lifestyle children needed.

And yet…

Leandro had an insane desire to whip this woman away, wrap her up in cotton wool and protect her because she was now the mother of his unborn child.

He stepped back, looked away, shaken to the core but channelling her up and then out, barely aware of telling his startled PA to block out all meetings for the remainder of the day.

Urged on by Leandro, Celia felt as though control had been whipped away from her.

She'd come to tell him what had needed to be told but after that? She'd vaguely assumed that a billionaire who had been frank about his views on commitment and marriage and everything that went with it would hardly have flung down the welcome mat at what she had to say. After that? Who knew? After that, her mind had been taken up with the ensuing way forward, breaking the news to her mum and dad, absorbing their disappointment, which would be hidden beneath their loving support. They would ask themselves how it was that she had made mistakes not once, but *twice*, and, this time, a mistake with long-reaching consequences.

They would wonder how it was that they had brought her up to respect the tradition of marriage and to value love and commitment only to get involved with a guy who had no interest in any of that.

The tangle of thoughts had stopped at Leandro's office door, like a messenger ringing a doorbell to deliver a package and then leaving.

So she was in a daze as she was ushered to an underground car park where she vaguely noted three high-end cars, all black, parked alongside one another.

He took the middle car, a low sleek sports car that purred into low-throated life as he slowly manoeuvred it out of the car park and into the London traffic.

'When did you find out?' Leandro glanced across to her before refocusing on the stop-start traffic.

'A couple of days ago,' Celia said unevenly.

'And have you told…anyone yet? Your parents?'

'I'm…working myself up to it. I thought… you should be the first to know, considering you're the father.'

'Thank you for that.'

'For what?' Celia laughed humourlessly. 'For being honest with you? Look, I'm not sure how much there is to talk about, Leandro. You forget we spent time together…long enough for me to know that this must be your worst nightmare come true. I've already told you that I don't expect anything from you.'

'And for that,' Leandro said quietly, again glancing across at her.

'For what?'

'For telling me that you don't expect anything from me.'

That stung. Celia's eyes glazed over and she stared out of the window in absolute silence, digesting what he'd said.

Of course he was grateful that she wasn't going to make a nuisance of herself. Did he think that she might have turned clingy and needy? She loved him but he didn't know that and he never would. She might have lost her heart to him, but she hadn't lost her dignity and she never would.

She almost laughed out loud when she thought about how he would have reacted if he'd known, not just that she was pregnant, but that she was in love with him! He would have strapped rockets to his ankles in his hurry to see the back of her.

So was he whipping her away to the privacy of his house to try and come to an arrangement whereby they worked out how she could become invisible?

No…even as Celia thought that, she knew, deep down, that that just wasn't the guy she had fallen for.

'We're here.'

Celia shook herself and took stock of the electric gates opening to a pale grey courtyard fringed with impeccably manicured grass. By London standards, it was huge for a house within easy reach of the city. The house itself was as modern as his manor estate in Scotland had been old and established, a marvel of sharp angles and banks of glass, all protected by high walls even though it was a quiet and tree-lined residential street.

She was ushered into a vast, cleverly arranged open-plan space, the sort of uber-sophisticated bachelor pad that would have cost a small fortune. The kitchen, to the left, looked over an island the size of a skating rink and behind which sat a vision of metal and chrome and marble. Ahead were various rooms, some behind doors and the living area was a sunken space sparsely furnished with pale tan leather and a white rug. A galleried landing, where the bedrooms were, she assumed, overlooked everything on the ground floor.

'Celia...' he guided her to the sitting area and waited as she gingerly perched on the edge of one of the immaculate leather sofas '... I thank you for telling me that you expect nothing from me because I can't think of any woman who wouldn't see this situation as a passport to asking a great deal from me. What can I get you to drink? Tea? Coffee? Are those things off limits for pregnant women?' He squatted next to her, then swerved to sit so close that his thigh was pressed against hers. 'Surely you know that the last thing I have any intention of doing is *nothing*.'

'What do you mean?'

'I mean you can trust me to do what needs

to be done. I am a man of honour, as you know, and I have every intention of doing the honourable thing. Neither you nor our child will want for anything. I'll take care of that.'

'You'll take care of that…' Celia parroted.

'It's a pretty scary time for you,' Leandro murmured as Celia continued to gape at him. 'You haven't told your parents and I'm guessing, when you say that you're *working up to that*, that you're privately apprehensive about what their reaction is going to be…maybe scared at what you might think will be inevitable disappointment.'

Celia dragged her eyes away with some effort. 'You have no idea what's going through my head, Leandro.'

Except he did, right down to the last detail, from the sounds of it.

'I might not have seen this coming,' Leandro admitted, 'but you're pregnant and there's no other option than for us to be married.'

Celia, who had been gaping before, now uttered a strangulated sound of complete shock. Her eyes widened. 'Get married? Get *married*? No! Leandro, we're not going to *get married*.'

'We are,' Leandro countered quietly and without a shred of doubt in his voice. 'I could give you a thousand reasons why. I could write a book on how beneficial it would be for our child to be raised with financial security and I speak from a position of experience. I could tell you that your traditional parents would welcome their only daughter getting married and settling down to raise a family, not having to go through the heartache of disappointment and anxious that they may have failed to provide you with the wherewithal to make sensible life choices. But the only reason that counts is this: when you have a child, it becomes time to put selfish concerns about your own happiness behind you because there's no room for that. Something else—' his voice hardened as he rose to his feet '—I learnt on my travels through life. I don't intend to be an absentee father because I don't happen to fit the bill when it comes to the life partner you had in mind, because this is not what either of us signed up for.'

There was intent behind his words but, more than that, a sincerity that made her realise that he would do everything it took to fulfil his fatherly obligations. He was a man who had no problem with a marriage of convenience. He had just left one behind. This was more of the same, if for a different reason.

How far would he go for the sake of honour and was that something she wanted to find out?

And how much would *she* sacrifice because she was in love with a guy who didn't love her back? The happiness of her own baby? Because she might not be able to deal with daily contact with Leandro? Was that something *she* wanted to put to the test?

'Can I think about it?' Celia murmured.

'You can think about it—' his voice was deadly serious '—but there will only be one answer I'm willing to accept...'

CHAPTER SEVEN

'I CAN'T BELIEVE IT. Have I said that already? Yes. I have. But it's…well, pet, you know the old saying…you spend a lifetime waiting for a bus and then two come along one after the other. First Dan and lovely, lovely Julie and now you and Leandro. You know your dad and I couldn't be happier…'

Celia made a game effort to smile. She and her mother were in the kitchen clearing away the dishes. Leandro and her father had remained in the sitting room for a while, bonding over a glass of port, which, for her father, could be classified as a celebration after-dinner drink, and had then retired for the night. Leandro had swanned into the kitchen, given her mother a hug and a peck on the cheek, effusively thanked her for the best roast dinner he had ever had, and announced that he would be heading up.

It had taken a little over a week for her to

summon up the necessary courage to make the trip to Shrewsbury so that she could break the joyful news to her parents.

A husband-to-be…a baby on the way…love at first sight…every romantic dream rolled into one with dizzying speed.

They had both patiently explained the situation with Julie and her engagement to Leandro as soon as they had arrived several hours earlier but, as it turned out, both her parents were already aware of the backstory.

Dan had told them all about the engagement of convenience and how it had crashed and burned when he and Julie had fallen in love.

'I would have told you,' Lizzie Drew had said sheepishly, 'but we'd only just about found out ourselves and I thought it best if Dan and Julie told you themselves. Cleared the air. I know they planned on meeting Leandro, but they wanted to reassure Julie's father first that he had nothing to worry about. It all seemed a bit of a muddle for me to start trying to dissect down the end of the line but now that you're both here…and, well! What a wonderful turn up for the books!'

As far as her mum was concerned, Celia discovered very quickly that her fairy story of meeting the guy of her dreams was every bit as romantic as Julie and Dan's had been.

The fact that Leandro had been prepared to marry a woman so that he could rescue her father from pain and penury already spoke volumes. There was already a halo on his head by the time they'd rung the doorbell.

And Leandro had not failed when it came to keeping the halo in place. He had gone full throttle with the charm and, over the course of dinner, Celia had watched her parents visibly melt.

If they had been favourably predisposed towards Leandro to start with, then, by the time the sticky toffee pudding was eaten, they had become full-time members of his fan club.

Not for one single second had either of them had any doubts that she and Leandro were in love.

The pregnancy had said it all.

They had such faith in her, and were so disingenuously convinced that their daughter would never fall pregnant unless love was involved because that was how she had been brought up, that the entire evening had been filled with teary-eyed smiles and congratulations and enthusiastic wedding planning.

Now, with the last dish finally washed and at a little after eleven, Celia felt as exhausted as if she'd run a marathon. She looked around the sparkling kitchen and wondered whether she could hang around for another couple of hours pointlessly wiping the counters, because arrangements on the sleeping front all seemed to be a bit of a nightmare.

'You go on up, Mum,' she said faintly as her mother headed to the kitchen door. 'I'll stay here…er…' she looked around her at the spotless kitchen with a hint of desperation '…and unload the dishwasher. You and Dad are leaving first thing in the morning for your cruise—you don't want to come down to a full dishwasher…'

Quite rightly, her mother looked a little startled at this suggestion.

'I wish you had come sooner, darling. I so would have liked to have spent longer going over all the wedding plans…you know… Dan's getting married but there's nothing like a mother and her daughter when it comes to weddings.'

'Well, like I mentioned, Mum…it's going to be a small wedding…all under the radar… literally just you, Dad, Dan and Julie and Julie's dad…piled into a register office…'

She smiled brightly while wondering how her life had veered so wildly off course from what she had always planned for herself.

The girl who had been saved from marrying the wrong guy was now marrying the wrong guy.

The girl who had thought she'd learned lessons had ended up learning nothing at all.

The girl who'd dreamt of a big white wedding, with all her friends and relatives there, was looking forward to a register office and an event that would be a formality, just a piece of paper signed legitimising the union she had been persuaded into. Not that it had taken much persuasion. Not only could she see things from Leandro's point of view... not only could she empathise with his need to provide two parents for his child where he had had one, but from her point of view, yes, a child should never pay for the mistakes of its parents.

If, in the years to come, their situation became insupportable, then that was another matter.

For the moment, as he had pointed out, they got along very well indeed and how, he had inserted deftly, would she ever be able to explain to their son or daughter that they had been denied the advantages of having both parents because she'd decided that she wouldn't give it a go?

Celia had seen the harshness on his beautiful

face and had known what he had been thinking. That his own mother hadn't been bothered and look at the legacy she had left behind.

But she knew that she had wandered into a minefield because everything had changed.

She hadn't been able to fault him. For the past week and a half, he had seen her three times and together, like business associates, they had hammered out their way forward.

He had listened to her concerns and had answered all of them, fairly and gently and with understanding. She had told him that there was no way she wanted to live in London.

'I can't imagine bringing up a child in the city,' she had admitted, looking around his spartan, urban space and wondering whether there could possibly be anywhere less suited to a child. 'I grew up in the country and I know it would be inconvenient, but if we get married, then we need to find a solution to that.'

He had agreed with alacrity. There was Surrey…there was Berkshire…there were countless towns and villages where she could find the space she needed, which would also be commutable to London.

'You can keep your shop here, in London,' he had said thoughtfully. 'Maybe leave the running of it to your assistants? And start afresh wherever we settle. I imagine the provinces might prove a very lucrative market for wedding dresses unless, of course, you want to pack in working altogether, which would be absolutely fine with me.'

Celia had hurriedly turned down that suggestion. The thought of being dependent for ever on someone who didn't love her and was only with her for the sake of the child they had conceived didn't sit well.

There were moments when she almost wished that he weren't quite so nice because *nice* was not what she wanted. She missed the Leandro who had looked at her with simmering passion, who had made love to her until she'd wanted to scream with pleasure. She missed the sexy, sensual familiarity that had grown between them during those magical days in Scotland, when they had been prisoners of the weather.

Now, he gave her respect and she didn't know what to do with it.

The guy who had huskily asked her to continue what they'd started when they returned to London had gone for good.

In his place was the guy who, undeniably, wanted to do the right thing and quite frankly would turn out to be a great dad.

But he no longer touched her. He kept his distance and that hurt even though she knew, in a muddled way, that touching would just add to the complications.

Was he assuming that, because this was a business arrangement for him, what they would have would be along the same lines as what he had agreed with Julie? An open marriage of sorts where she would discreetly overlook any misdemeanours?

Or was he just biding his time? He might genuinely believe that two parents were better than one, but maybe, subconsciously, he also knew that a divorced guy had a lot more rights than one who had never married.

Was he playing a waiting game? He certainly no longer had any interest in her on the physical level.

It was a subject Celia dared not broach because of the worms that might start crawling out of the can.

Did she really want him to kindly tell her that she wasn't his type after all? That what they'd had had worked in Scotland, where reality was something they had left behind? That it just wasn't something, on reflection, that could survive the light of day?

Did she want him to know how much she missed him? No, she didn't.

They would marry and who knew—it was possible that seeing him up close and personal all the time would put paid to the hold he had over her. How long could one person carry on loving someone who wasn't interested?

The house was quiet by the time she made her way up to the bedroom that her mother had lovingly made up for them, right down to flowers in the vase on the chest of drawers and some kind of scent that filled the room with the smell of cedarwood.

She quietly pushed open the door to a semi-darkened room and Leandro on the bed and, suddenly, she was on red-hot alert, her senses quivering with forbidden excitement. The horse might have bolted and it might have been futile trying to bolt the stable door, but right now there was no comfort in the fact that they had been lovers.

She felt his dangerous presence and shivered.

'You're on the bed.' Celia folded her arms and stared down at Leandro, who returned her gaze, unperturbed.

He was half naked and she hoped that the nudity didn't extend beyond what she could see because she didn't think her blood pressure could take it.

'Where else am I supposed to be?'

'Leandro,' she muttered, but she could feel her fingers digging into her arms, 'this isn't going to work.'

'Why not?'

'Because…because this isn't what we're about now!'

No, Leandro thought. Under normal circumstances, wouldn't this have been a good outcome? A marriage of convenience, admittedly, but one with the bonus of hot sex. With or without the hot sex, however, it was a union he had been determined to cement. The fierceness of what he felt for this unborn baby astonished him, but he wasn't going to pretend it didn't exist, and, that being the case, his mind had leapt several steps ahead, to a scenario in which they went their separate ways, sharing custodial rights.

A child toing and froing from one house to another. Different wardrobes in different places, treading a thin line between what was diplomatic to say to one parent in the absence of the other.

Eventually, another man would come on the scene. How long before that other man became central to his child's life? How long before *his* flesh and blood started calling *another guy* his *dad*?

Right there and then, Leandro had known that no way was that ever going to be allowed to happen on his watch. And more than that… more than all those plausible scenarios was the uneasy recognition that she was pulling away from him. Hell! He didn't want to care but he was finding that he did. He didn't want her distance. He wanted…what? Could it be the ease of connection they had had before things had become complicated? Before a future he had never considered became the present with which they both had to deal?

Now here they were.

'This room,' he told her, voice cooling, 'is the size of a matchbox. You want me to sleep on the ground? I'll sleep on the ground.' How ironic that they were now in the most intimate situation possible and yet she couldn't bear the thought of sharing her bed with him. 'And what if they poke their heads in and find the pair of love birds not sharing the same bed?'

'They're leaving at the crack of dawn to-morrow morning. They'd never know.'

'Fine.' Leandro shrugged and made to fling aside the duvet.

'Okay. No. They…it might be hard to ex-plain if they popped in to say goodbye be-fore they left.'

'Yes. After the effusive welcome we received, there might have been disappointment all round if they thought we'd ended the evening on a raging argument serious enough to send us shooting off in separate bedrooms. What's the problem with sharing a bed? Have I tried to lay a single finger on you since you came back into my life? Have I given you any reason to believe that I'm anything other than a decent guy trying to do the decent thing, which doesn't include forcing himself on a woman who's not interested?'

Their eyes tangled, his darkly brooding, holding her gaze until she was the first to look away.

If he'd hoped to force a response from her, then it hadn't been forthcoming and he was annoyed with himself for trying to corner her into saying something, *anything* that would let him know what exactly was going on behind that guarded exterior.

Foremost wasn't the crazy issue that he was still attracted to her. It wasn't even the realisation that he had become the very man he had always sworn he never would…a man vulnerable to someone else's decisions. First and foremost and the only thing that mattered was the knowledge that she was having his baby and he was going to marry her, going to be a full-time father with none of the hopeless complications associated with any kind of joint custody.

Sure, joint custody would always be a damn sight better than what *he* had had as a kid, but it still would never be in the same league as a child having both parents there.

He noted the tic in her neck and the steady blush that invaded her cheeks and he wondered whether she was trying to work out how to knock him back without getting into a pointless war of words.

'No, of course you haven't.' Celia tilted her chin at a mutinous, defensive angle. 'I just thought that it might be a bit awkward… It's not a very big bed…'

'Feel free to barricade yourself behind the cushions but trust me…if our bodies touch during the night, then I assure you it will be purely accidental.'

Which, Celia thought with such a sharp stab of pain that she momentarily felt faint, pretty much said it all. Accidental touching where before there had been touching with intent, with intent and passion and desire and, she'd sometimes thought, more affection and tenderness than he was probably even aware of.

'I would never,' Leandro said gravely, his voice warmer, 'do anything that might make you feel in the least bit uncomfortable. If it would make you feel a little...less awkward, I can head down to the kitchen and spend a couple of hours working, give you time to fall asleep in peace.'

'It's okay,' Celia muttered, flushing. 'I'll get changed and of course it's not a problem sharing the bed. I... I apologise for—'

'Forget it!' He waved his hand dismissively. 'This is new for the both of us. Let's put this kind of thing down to teething problems.'

She did.

She took her time showering unnecessarily and then she took her time applying some night cream and then doing a few deep-breathing exercises before she returned to the bedroom in the most conservative nightwear she had, long bottoms and a short-sleeved top firmly buttoned up.

She slept. Soundly. If their bodies *accidentally* touched, then she wasn't aware of it.

She woke at five, her senses alert to her parents up and about and trying to be as quiet as they could.

Next to her, Leandro was still asleep, the covers half off, his muscular, bronzed body so compellingly beautiful that she remained frozen and in awe, drinking in the sight and luxuriating in the freedom of appreciating him, of not having to hide her love because he was sleeping.

Then she slid off the bed, tiptoed out of the bedroom and only detoured via the bathroom to shove on her bathrobe so that she could go and wish her parents a good holiday.

They might have been in a state of simmering excitement about their departure but not so excited that they didn't have time to repeat the mantra of how wonderful they thought Leandro was. So much better suited to her than Martin had been, for all Martin's sterling qualities. Celia marvelled that her parents could both misread Leandro so completely but, then again, the guy could charm the birds from the trees and he had dazzled them both, maybe just the way he'd dazzled *her*.

It was nearly an hour before she headed back to the bedroom but still only just after six in the morning and she half expected Leandro to still be asleep, but when she quietly pushed open the bedroom door, heartened by the fact that the lights hadn't been switched on, she was shocked to find that the bed was empty and Leandro was perched on a chair by the window. He had pulled open the curtains just enough for her eyes to quickly adjust to the fact that he had changed into jeans and a tee shirt. His long legs were stretched out at an angle and next to him…

Draped half on, half off the stout chest of drawers she had used ever since she'd been a kid…

Celia's mouth dropped open and she took a couple of faltering steps forward.

'What…what's this doing out?'

'Tell me about it.'

'You've been rummaging in my wardrobe?'

'Hunting down a face towel. Thought there might be a stash there. You never said you'd hung onto your wedding dress from years ago.'

'Because that was none of your business!' But she walked towards the dress, covered in its voluminous mothproof cover, and gazed down for a few seconds at it.

When she rested her hand on it, she didn't flinch as he covered it with his own.

Leandro watched her closely.

He'd vaguely been rooting around for a face towel but the truth was that he'd heard her sidle out of the bedroom and had known that she'd been heading down to chat to her parents before they left on their holiday.

They'd slept in her bedroom. There was stuff everywhere, from the pictures in the frames on the dressing table to the old board games in a stack on the shelf above the chest of drawers.

He'd leapt out of bed, slung on some clothes and taken his time looking at the pictures, stories of a happy childhood. He'd only peered into the wardrobe because he'd just happened to be standing in front of it and his curiosity about Celia had been piqued by the mementoes all around him.

And the wedding dress had been impossible to miss because it was the only thing in the cupboard and it took up so much space.

He knew that she didn't pine for her ex. She might have been hurt but she had never registered any lingering pain when she'd mentioned him.

But that didn't mean that the experience had killed off all her dreams. She'd planned for the big white wedding and she'd hung onto the dress because it had been a reminder of what she had longed for.

In a flash, Leandro realised just how much she was willing to sacrifice for the sake of a child neither of them had reckoned on.

Not just her hopes of finding Mr Perfect, after she'd almost married Mr Imperfect, but all the other things that went with that. The courtship...the planning for the big day...

the confetti and photos and speeches and the driving off to the romantic honeymoon. The way she now rested her small hand on that dress and the wistful look in her eyes said it all and something inside Leandro twisted.

'I'm not going to force your hand,' he said roughly. Their eyes met and he nodded at the wedding dress. 'If you're still holding onto dreams, then I don't want to be the one to trample all over them.'

'That's not what you said to me a few days ago. A few days ago you made it clear that marriage was the only solution as far as you were concerned.'

'It still is but I have no intention of getting what I want by using a whip.'

Celia raised her eyebrows at this change in tune, then she sighed, thought of what life would look like without him in it, now that she had reconciled herself to marrying him.

It wasn't an attractive picture.

Disentangling her parents from the happy-ever-after fairy-tale ending was just the cherry on top. The truth was that she had guiltily found herself painting unrealistic pictures in her head about life with Leandro.

Of course he didn't love her! Good heavens, he no longer even wanted to come near her physically! There were so many problems associated with those two things, but hadn't there been just a tiny bloom of *possibilities* cutting a forbidden path through all of that? Hadn't a little voice carried on saying, however much she'd tried to shut it down, that who knew what lay around the corner...?

'You're not,' she confessed. 'So I really didn't think that we would end up...well, *here*, when I came to tell you about the pregnancy, but I agree that two parents are usually better than one and you've met Mum and Dad. That was how I was brought up. So you're not forcing my hand. If I really and truly didn't want to go through with it, then I wouldn't. And for the wedding dress? I hung onto it...' She paused and glanced down, noting with surprise his hand on hers and quietly slipping hers free '...because it was the first one I ever tried my hand at after I finished my course. I...it's not even properly finished, so it isn't as though I could sell it...'

Her voice petered out and the silence hung heavily between them for a few seconds.

She didn't know where this was going and she had no idea what was coming next, so she was shocked when he said, voice low and even, 'We've talked about a lot of things, by which I mean, we've gone through all the reasons why we've decided on…doing what needs to be done for the sake of this baby. We've agreed on where we could live and the money side of things…but on a less… formal level, you're going to be giving a lot up for this.'

'As are you.'

'We also,' he said neutrally, 'find ourselves in the unique position of being in the most intimate situation possible without the benefit of really knowing one another.'

'I…' Celia was hurt because she'd thought they'd got to know one another well over that short space of time. She'd told him things she'd never told anyone else. Had she been a complete fool in thinking that perhaps it might have been the same for him? Just a little? 'I…yes, I suppose you're right…'

'To make this really work, maybe we should take some time out together.'

'You think that because I didn't tell you about the wedding dress you don't know me?'

'How much do we know one another?' His voice was a low, lazy drawl.

In truth, Leandro realised that he had been more unsettled by that wedding dress in the cupboard than he'd thought. Of course it had made him realise what she was giving up, all the intangible things she was saying good-bye to.

He patted himself on the back because that showed a magnanimous side to him of which he was proud, even though the emotional response was unusual enough to floor him.

But now that he considered it in a little more depth, he wondered whether her nostalgia for romance would leave ajar a door through which she would eventually be tempted to enter. Would she want to see what was on the other side?

He would take things back a bit, he'd determined. They'd skipped a lot of steps in the process she'd probably spent her whole life looking forward to. He'd met her parents, had been charmed by them, had seen them for the traditional sort who truly believed in the power of love. He didn't get it, but what he *did* get was the power of sex and that was something they had had in abundance.

So she had given him the cold shoulder when he'd suggested they continue. Maybe she'd had big dreams of walking off into a rosy sunset arm in arm with some guy who probably didn't exist, whom she might or might not meet one fine day and to whom she would give her heart.

But they were here now and something

about her alarm at sharing the bed with him the night before had nudged something inside him. Was she as indifferent to him as she wanted to be? Or was there still the same simmering attraction inside her that, if enticed, would blow hot and fierce as it had done before?

She might not welcome a reaction that didn't suit her ideals but if they were to be married…? Then the world turned on its axis, didn't it?

Thoughts of seduction, let loose from the cage in which they had been confined, roared out with the power of a sudden burning conflagration.

Seduction rarely involved the prosaic. They had done prosaic, insofar as prosaic could exist in their current situation.

'Once we're married, whatever the timeline, the pregnancy will be further along,' he murmured. 'You might even find it difficult to travel anywhere…'

'Travel anywhere?' Celia looked at him with open bewilderment. 'I know my car is small,' she said, 'but, actually, I *will* still be able to get around in it! Even if I grow to the size of a barrage balloon, I can just push the seat back a bit and travelling isn't going to be some kind of dicing-with-misfortune experience, Leandro. I'm not going to be an invalid just because I'm having a baby!'

'What's the state of your passport?' he mused, by way of response, and Celia frowned.

'I have one. Why do you ask?'

'I may be realistic,' he responded wryly, 'when it comes to finding solutions to problems, but I'm not completely without finesse. Most married couples go on honeymoon.'

'We're not most married couples.'

'In the eyes of your parents, we are, wouldn't you agree?' He waited a heartbeat knowing that there was no argument she could use against that. 'They would hardly expect us to get married, as the loved-up couple they believe us to be, for me to promptly return to work without even paying lip service to my new bride...'

There were so many words in that sentence that were at odds with what actually existed between them that Celia's head was in a whirl and yet, treacherously, she clung to those words with the desperation of a complete idiot. *Loved-up couple...new bride...a honeymoon befitting those things...*

He was only stating the obvious, wasn't he?

They *had* put on a united front. They had come as the bearer of glad tidings and her parents had not doubted otherwise. Many times, Leandro's arm had rested across her shoulders...around her waist...his fingers lightly feathering her wrist...his thigh brushing hers as they had sat together on the sofa in the sitting room.

She had been unbearably *aware* of each and every one of those little intimate gestures because she was so unbearably aware of *him*. Her parents, of course, would have been equally aware of each and every one of those gestures. Her mother was eagle-eyed when it came to things like that.

Celia was sure that her mum would be nursing some disappointment about the size of the wedding. She would have wanted planning and hats and showing off her daughter to all her friends in the village. But she hadn't said a word. However, if there were to be no honeymoon and nothing at all to mark the event as something joyous and to be celebrated, then how would she feel?

Would a pretence of a honeymoon be necessary?

'I suppose we could pretend to do something.' She frowned, staring off into the distance, and Leandro did his best not to grit his teeth in pure frustration.

Was there a woman as challenging as the one now chewing her lip and staring off as though waiting for divine inspiration? Was it utterly arrogant and egotistic of him to think that there were very few women who wouldn't have leapt at everything he had offered instead? The ring? And all the benefits that came with that? Which, quite frankly, were more than generous?

'We could. What,' he asked with an edge of genuine curiosity, 'did you have in mind?'

'Well, we could hide out at your place...'

Leandro burst out laughing and, when he'd sobered up, he gazed at her with amusement. 'When this breaks, there'll be some press coverage. I'm a billionaire. I'm not saying the paparazzi are going to be stalking us in the hope of a juicy story, but I'm well enough known in financial and society circles for some interest. If they discover that we've put it about that we're heading off to exotic climes on a pre-baby-being-born honeymoon only to discover that we're both lurking under the bed at my London place, then I can't think what will be made of that.'

'Exotic climes?'

Leandro shrugged. 'The world is full of some exceptionally lovely outposts.'

'So you're thinking we actually go some-where.'

'Leave it to me. I'll sort everything out.' He grinned. 'And you can relax. You're pregnant. Pregnant women are supposed to take it easy. I'll make sure you don't have a minute's stress.'

Celia gaped and blinked. Was he kidding? A honeymoon with this guy so that they could *get to know one another* and he was guaranteeing her a stress-free experience? What planet was he on?

But of course she knew.

He wanted to make sure they entered this new arrangement as friends, and friends surely didn't stress about spending time in one another's company. Did they?

Except for her...

When she thought about being away with him, she felt faint, but he was already rising to his feet, getting ready to start the day, and she knew, with a sinking heart, that what he wanted he was going to get.

CHAPTER EIGHT

CELIA'S IDEA OF the perfect honeymoon involved white sands and blue sea and lazy cocktails on a beach and being somewhere where you could easily imagine that the rest of the world didn't actually exist. Even after she and Martin had parted company, she could remember guiltily and longingly gazing at faraway destinations in magazines, where sun, sea and sand were the only 'S's to be had, without that other one, *stress*, rearing its ugly head and spoiling everything.

By the time they'd returned to London the previous afternoon, *stress* at whatever Leandro had planned had definitely been high on the agenda as she'd churned over in her head the prospect of going on a pseudo honeymoon with him.

She'd made an effort to find out what he had in mind, but he had told her to just make sure her passport was up to date and her summer wardrobe was up and running.

Then he'd looked at her, a quick, sidelong glance as his powerful car ate up the motorway miles, and said thoughtfully, 'I think a shopping trip might be in order.'

Why fight it?

The consequences of accepting his offer of marriage had been beginning to sink in.

The altruistic *rightness* of doing the best for the baby they now shared hid a network of uncomfortable realities.

His wealth was staggering and while she had every intention of continuing her own business, adapting and adjusting as necessary, she would essentially be the recipient of immense financial comfort.

How could she dig her heels in and fight that? He wanted the best for his child and she would be tugged along in the undertow.

'Really?' She'd greeted his pensive observation with a half-hearted lack of enthusiasm. 'I have summer clothes.'

'What?'

'I said I already have perfectly fine summer clothes.'

'No. *What* summer clothes do you have?'

Celia had bristled, but had then remembered what her summer wardrobe consisted of and said, truthfully, 'I think I have some shorts and a couple of dresses.' The truth was that she had the sort of clothes designed to hide behind. Baggy shirts and loose-fitting dresses and everything in muted colours that allowed her to fade into the background.

'We're going to be getting married,' Leandro had pointed out. 'You're going to have to dress the part.'

'*Dress the part?* Do you think I'm some kind of Barbie doll, Leandro? What world do you live in where you really imagine that women should dress to fit in with a guy?'

'Actually...' Leandro had been sidetracked '...you'd be surprised how many women enjoy shopping for expensive clothes. They rarely have to be forced into it kicking and screaming. But,' he'd continued reasonably, 'that wasn't what I was getting at.'

'No?'

'If we go anywhere expensive, you're going to be ill at ease in clothes that make you feel self-conscious. Besides, has it occurred to you that I might actually want to treat my bride-to-be to a new wardrobe? Jewellery? Holidays? A new car...?'

Bride-to-be in name only, Celia had thought. 'I don't need a new car.'

'Stop arguing with me all the time.'

'If I don't happen to agree with what you're saying, it doesn't mean that I'm arguing with you.'

At which point he'd burst out laughing and told her that he would collect her the following morning at ten sharp from her house.

So here she was now. She was no wiser as to the destination of this honeymoon and locked into a morning shopping with Leandro.

She was far from beginning to show yet but, even so, her first words as she settled into the back of his chauffeur-driven car were, 'It's silly to spend a lot of money on clothes that are only going to fit me for a few weeks—by the time summer rolls round over here, I'll be as big as a whale.'

'And a good morning to you as well, Celia. Good night's sleep? I wouldn't have to do this trip out if you'd simply listened to me and moved into my place. It's not like your parents' house where you would be forced to share a bed with me. You would be able to have your pick of rooms.'

When he had suggested that, Celia had instantly turned him down on the grounds that there was no need.

'Where are you taking me?' she now asked and he grinned.

* * *

'You make that sound as though I'm ferrying you for a day out of pure torture.'

'I hate shopping.'

'I believe you've mentioned that to me once.'

'Have I?'

'It may have been post-coital conversation in the early hours of the morning when we were in Scotland.' His voice was husky and amused. When he thought of those intimate moments in the stillness of a snowy night, when they had talked about anything and everything, he could feel his libido rising to the occasion and reminding him of just how much he was going to enjoy seducing her back into his bed.

More and more, he got the tantalising sensation that what she wanted to box away was still there, a simmering physical pull that matched his. Why was she so keen to deny it? Was it because she'd come to the conclusion that to indulge in sex with him was no longer acceptable despite the situation they were in because she needed an emotional attachment he was incapable of giving? Had she succumbed once and decided that once was enough? Had she thought it through at all? Underneath all that speculation lay the uneasy notion that she subconsciously saw herself walking away from a marriage in search of the fairy-story ending, maybe not immediately but sooner rather than later.

Was he being over-imaginative? Leandro didn't know because she was the very essence of everything that was mysterious about the opposite sex even though she could be as transparent as a pane of glass.

If she wanted to lock those memories away then he'd determined that he wasn't going to let her and he wished he could see her face now as he dropped that perfectly innocuous remark in a voice that was easy-going, casual and reeking of innocence, but he didn't want to make a point of it.

'Don't worry. I guarantee you'll enjoy the experience and to answer your question— Selfridges.'

Celia lapsed into silence. Post-coital conversation… She wished he hadn't reminded her of those because how she had luxuriated in them, loving the darkness and the quiet and the lazy chat that was so easy and languid in bed, naked bodies pressed together, warm and content.

Overwhelmed by a sudden wave of sadness for having made the mistake of falling cra-

zily in love with a guy who was incapable of
loving anyone, she blinked and stared out of
the window at yet another grey day.

She wasn't aware of Leandro reaching out
until she felt the curl of his fingers around
hers and when she swung round to look at
him, she was bowled over by the gentleness
on his face.

'It's going to be okay,' he said roughly.

In that very instant, Celia made her decision.

She would never find the love she wanted
with Leandro but she *would* have support
and affection. It might not have been on her
wish list when she was young and filled with
dreams about her future, but she was going to
marry him and they were having a baby and
it could have been a whole lot worse.

And if he didn't and never would love her?

The option of pulling back, of trying not
to go further down the road of giving him
her heart, now seemed naïve and futile. What
would happen in that scenario? He would
eventually drift away from her. He would
turn to other women to find physical closeness. She had debated telling him that she
wouldn't marry unless he promised not to
stray, but had known that that would have
been crazy unless they became lovers once

again. Not knowing what to do, she had remained paralysed, but now...?

Those fingers entwined with hers would have to be enough. She would never tell him how she really felt because she would always want to hang onto her dignity, but she could no longer fight the hold he had over her.

Was it the same for him?

He hadn't come near her since they had left Scotland, but if she didn't risk finding out whether there was any semblance of attraction left between them, then she would regret the omission for ever.

She squeezed his hand without looking at him and then left her fingers linked with his. Finally, she turned and smiled weakly.

'If you say so.'

'We're here.' He nodded to the busy entrance.

Celia breathed in long and deep and together they headed into the department store.

She'd reached a crossroads and was going to make the very best of where she was. She was going to love this man and if he hurt her, then she would accept the body blow.

They went directly to the designer floor. Celia had only been into Selfridges a couple of times and never anywhere near the designer section, which was out of bounds moneywise for her.

He held her hand and moved with confidence, ignoring eager looks on salespeople's faces, asking her what sort of things she liked to wear and then telling her that anything baggy was out of the question.

'Why?'

'Why would you hide your figure?' He slid appreciative eyes across to her and she blushed. 'It's amazing.'

She remembered the way he'd made her feel. Sexy and beautiful and provocative. He'd opened up a whole new side to her and it was exciting to think that she might go down that road again.

Would she?

She could feel his body language and it made her bloom somewhere deep inside with the slow burn of desire.

'Can I ask you something?' Celia stopped and looked up at him, suddenly anxious to find out why, having been so scrupulous in avoiding touching her ever since she'd shown up, he was now giving off signals that he wanted her after all.

Had he reconciled himself to taking what he thought might now be on offer? Even though he might have been happy to shrug her off before? Easy come, easy go?

She wanted him. She was in love with him. But was she so in love and did she want him so much that she would be happy to be considered as better than nothing? Would her self-esteem ever recover? But then she thought of them living separate lives, growing more and more distant from one another over time, holding herself in a state of frozen limbo because she didn't want to have sex with someone who couldn't give her the love she craved. How satisfying would that be?

There were few people around them, but she still shuffled him away from the main drag and towards the side.

'Do I have a choice of answer?' Leandro asked cautiously and Celia chewed her lower lip and shook her head, which was honest enough.

'You haven't…come near me ever since I told you about the pregnancy…'

'Come again?'

'I got the impression…that…er…' His look of bewilderment made her stumble over her words but then his expression cleared and he looked at her seriously.

'You made it clear that you weren't interested in prolonging what we had,' Leandro said bluntly. 'I got the message loud and clear so when you showed up, I was hardly going to take that as a green light to start making a move on you, was I?'

He tilted her chin so that she was looking at him, her clear green eyes hesitant.

'Do you know what my mission in life is?' he asked, his voice teasing, which brought all sorts of tingly sensations racing through her, making her squirm in a very pleasurable way.

'What?' Her voice was breathless and she was mesmerised by the glint in his eyes.

'To just get you to feel more confident about yourself.'

'Of course I'm confident!'

Leandro looked at her wryly. 'How could you think that I would want you one minute and then be so turned off you the next that I don't want to come near you?'

Celia shrugged. 'Men change their minds.'

'I don't. There's such a thing as respecting someone's choices.' He was tempted to ask her why *she* had found it so easy to dismiss what they'd enjoyed but he already knew. She'd been looking for Love and happy to relegate the fun they'd had to the history books.

Except fate had had other things in mind.

But he still turned her on and maybe she

was seeing things from his point of view now. A baby and a marriage and the bonus of great sex to keep the wheels oiled.

Love might not be part of the equation but that didn't mean that everything then became a lost cause. Life was seldom a case of all or nothing.

She'd forgotten the value of fun somewhere along the line and he was surprised at how relieved and frankly *overjoyed* he felt at the thought that she had come round to his way of thinking.

'So,' he purred silkily, 'shall we get down to the drudgery of shopping for an entire new wardrobe for you? Money no object?' He wagged his finger sternly at her. 'And don't even think about quibbling about that one...'

Celia had always loathed the business of buying clothes. Of course, Leandro had a point. When you lacked confidence in your body, when you looked in the mirror and mostly saw room for improvement, then trying on clothes became a chore.

But now she was imbued with such a sense of heady sexiness that she threw herself into the task with gusto. She forgot about the fact that most of the stuff came with price tags that made her eyes water.

Anticipation at what she had given herself permission to do gave an edge to the remainder of the day. Every sideways glance was thrilling, every brush of his hand against her sent a rush of adrenaline through her system.

Celia could barely remember what exactly she had chosen for herself because her mind had been racing ahead to what lay in store.

A night with Leandro, wrapped in his arms, her body singing to the drumbeat of his love-making.

She knew she stocked up on three dresses, some shorts, some tee shirts that were as soft as silk and even some strappy shoes and sandals. She bought stuff she would never have chosen for herself in a million years, tops that showed off her generous breasts and dresses that skimmed her thighs and delicate shoes that reminded her that she had very pretty feet and slender ankles.

They held hands, had some lunch and, in true billionaire style, he had his chauffeur stop so that the shopping could be dumped in the boot of his car. No inconvenient traipsing through the store weighed down by bags.

They were in the back of his car and heading to her place so that she could *fling a few things in a suitcase and make it quick because he was going crazy* when it occurred to Celia that he still hadn't told her where, exactly, they would be going.

'Dubai.'

'I've always wanted to go,' she confessed.

'It's busy. Had I known that we would…' he eyed the closed partition and lowered his voice to a seductive purr '…be spending a week removing one another's clothing and getting reacquainted with what's underneath, I would have definitely opted for something a little less frantic.'

'Thank you,' Celia said simply, then she looked away because there was way too much her eyes could tell him that her head warned her not to say.

The casual purchase of a wardrobe of designer clothes, a shopping trip where price tags weren't consulted because money didn't matter, should have prepared her for the lavish experience of travelling with a billionaire a mere three days later, but Celia was still shocked at the mind-blowing opulence of luxury travel.

They flew first. People fawned and practically pleaded to bring food and drink, whatever they wanted. There were massages on tap should they want…manicures and pedicures at the snap of a finger…

The sofas strewn here and there in artful symmetry were deep and comfortable and there were USB ports everywhere because nearly everyone in the spacious, airy lounge was a businessperson.

There was an air-conditioned limo with privacy windows waiting for them when they landed and they were ushered out with the sort of respect reserved for visiting dignitaries.

'I guess you come here often? Why do people know who you are?'

'No need to whisper, Celia. We're not in a library. And this is just the level of service that happens when you get to a certain financial position. Admittedly, I've met the Sheikh a few times in the course of business. You'll be pleased to hear that I've turned down his dinner invitation at his palace. We're here for a week and I intend to spend every second of the week in your company and your company alone.'

Leandro meant every word of that. He had barely been able to focus on work because having her back in his bed had taken up all his waking thoughts.

Sex had never ruled his life. He had never had a problem prioritising what was important, which was the thing that gave him financial security, the thing that saved him from the fate of his father. He had discovered, to his bemusement, that that paled into insignificance with Celia back on the scene.

He felt that it was all tied up with the fact that she was having his baby. No woman had ever occupied that spot in his life before and, while he had never thought about it, he now felt a depth of protectiveness that overruled everything else.

He couldn't stop looking at her. Right now, she was pink from the surge of heat outside the airport and her hair was in its usual disarray, rebelling against the clips she had pushed in to control it, begging to be released.

There was not an ounce of artificiality about her. She looked left to right and left to right as the limo left the airport towards the five-star hotel his PA had booked for him.

He reached to clasp her hand and she shot him an open, delighted smile.

'This is amazing,' she confessed. 'There weren't a huge amount of holidays growing up and when I left home to open my business, there just wasn't the cash to indulge in going abroad.'

'I never went on holiday either, as a child,' Leandro confided. 'It's why I never take any of this for granted, however much I'm used to it. I was propelled into private education thanks to Charles and I learned quickly how to survive in that small pond where the rich and famous swim.'

'How?'

'You need to have a killer instinct and when you come from nothing, you need to be better, faster and smarter than the kids who come from moneyed backgrounds. You have to make sure you don't give anyone an advantage over you.'

'A lonely life,' Celia murmured and Leandro flushed and looked away for a few seconds.

'I've never considered myself lonely,' he said crisply, holding her gaze for a moment and then briefly looking down. 'If anything, when I went to boarding school, I would say there were way too many people around.'

Celia half smiled and reached to squeeze his hand. 'I'll bet.'

Her eyes were warm and, suddenly disoriented, Leandro heard himself say gruffly, 'I admit I was lonely…sometimes.' Then he shrugged, astonished at that confidence. 'Kids adapt.' He dealt her a gentle smile. 'I'm just glad ours won't have to.'

'I might need to do a lot of adapting.' Celia laughed. 'I never saw myself living anywhere but a modest little house with a bit of a garden and enough space for a decent workroom.'

So the conversation moved on. They arrived not long after at the resort, which turned out to be a breathtakingly elegant compound located on the crisp white shores of Jumeirah Beach. It was big enough to get lost in and yet they were greeted, once out of the car, with impeccable efficiency. Celia lagged behind, awestruck by the opulence. Acres of marble floor and a dazzling abundance of chandeliers and gold-leaf ceilings nudged alongside warm earthy tones, a visual reminder that this palatial five-star resort owed its existence to the splendour of the sand and desert in which it resided. The searing heat was left behind as it was beautifully cool inside and busy with people coming and going. Many were tourists but many were also locals, wearing the impressive, traditional dress, white tunics and headscarves.

She half listened to the spiel the hotel receptionist was imparting as she went through the formalities of checking them in, then she smiled and said, deferentially, that perhaps

Mr Diaz already knew what there was to know as he had been there already.

'And our esteemed Royal Highness, the Sheikh, sends you his best,' she murmured, eyes lowered.

This was like no hotel Celia had ever been in, not that she had been in very many, and she followed Leandro in a daze as he confidently led the way to the bank of lifts purring up and down, disgorging people into the plush foyer and transporting ones on their way back to their rooms.

She could understand why he had chosen this place for a honeymoon that wasn't supposed to have been a real honeymoon. If the aim had been for them to get to at least know one another a bit better, without any atmosphere of romance to muddy the waters, then it couldn't have been better. Lavish and big enough to be impersonal, vibrant without the danger of intimacy lurking in secluded corners and cosy nooks and crannies.

They were whooshed out into a huge, ornately carpeted corridor with just a handful of doors guarding the most expensive of the suites.

'Wow.' That was all Celia could say as the heavy door was pushed open and she walked into a vast open space, all white, from the sprawling U-shaped leather suite to the pale rug on which it sat.

To one side, there was a magnificent circular glass table, big enough to seat eight, and directly in front was a bank of glass to which she was drawn.

The city twinkled far and away and beneath them. She rested her hands on the floor-to-ceiling glass and looked out and then shivered as she saw Leandro's reflection behind her.

He reached, flattening his palms on either side of hers, locking her in and sending goosebumps racing through her.

The thrill of flirting and the anticipation of where all that flirting was going to lead made her weak at the knees. She turned within the loop of his outstretched arms so that her back was against the glass and she stared up at him, breathing fast, her mouth parted in invitation.

He was wearing a light-coloured shirt, cuffed to the elbows, and low-slung chinos and she undid the buttons of the shirt and pushed her hands to feel the hardness of his chest, roughened with dark hair. She circled her fingers over his flat nipples and felt his sharp intake of breath. She tugged the shirt free of the trousers. His dark eyes held hers and she liked that because she could see the heat of desire burning in the depths, turning her on, fuelling her with the confidence that had been shorn away when she had thought that he no longer wanted her.

'I've wanted to touch you all day,' he rasped, one hand still planted on the glass while the other did to her what she was doing to him, pushed under the silk blouse to find the front clasp of her bra, which he undid with proficiency.

Her breasts fell full and soft, released from their restraints, and Leandro flung back his head, nostrils flared, eyes half closed as he cupped her breasts in his hands and massaged them.

With a groan he roughly undid the buttons, tugged her blouse free of the matching silk culottes, felt her wriggle against him, unzipping and pulling down, as frantic as he was.

They barely made it to the bedroom.

Clothes were shed on the way, a trail of discarded items that followed them into one of the three rooms, which was dominated by a super-king-size bed complete with drapery.

Celia vaguely took stock of all of this. Yes, she was aware of the size of the bedroom, the pale voile at the windows, the lush deep blue of the carpet and the sleek glossiness of the built-in furniture, but that was all on the periphery of her vision.

Really, she only had eyes for the man who was now standing back, looking at her with such hot longing in his eyes that she wanted to swoon.

They were both naked. She dimly remembered kicking off her panties. The cool air-conditioning made her nipples stiffen.

'I've missed you,' Leandro half moaned.

My body, Celia knew. Where *she* missed his familiarity and the wonderful essence of him, *he* missed her body, missed the sex.

It was something she would have to accept and accept it she would.

Her love was so entwined with lust and desire that she knew that they could never be untangled.

She sighed softly and her eyelids fluttered as he curved his hands smoothly over her waist and then he knelt at her feet and breathed her in.

He smoothed his hand over her belly and kissed it and then he gently eased her legs apart.

Oh, how she had missed this!

She arched back and reached out to clutch at one of the wooden posts of the bed. Then she lifted her leg, resting it on the mattress so that she could accommodate his exploring tongue working its way along her clitoris, teasing it into stiff arousal.

Her fingers curled into his dark hair. When she looked down with slumberous eyes, she was further turned on by the sight of him, moving against her, between her thighs.

He eased a finger into her, two fingers, and between his tongue and his mouth and those fingers, Celia could no longer hold on.

She came fast and hard, spasming against his mouth, her whole body convulsing with the mind-blowing pleasure of her orgasm. She barely recognised the guttural sounds leaving her mouth, but she could feel the hot, prickly flush of the blood rushing through her, as searing as fire.

The strength of her orgasm left her as weak as a kitten but she was still startled when he lifted her off her feet, as though she weighed nothing, and gently put her on the bed.

Their eyes tangled and she could feel her body begin to shift back into gear, could feel that want seep through her. It was an ache between her legs that made her want to rub them together.

'You are every man's dream,' Leandro husked, bending to suckle on one nipple, which turned want back into mindless craving with supersonic speed.

'That's the nicest thing anyone's ever said to me.' She laughed softly and tugged him so that they were looking at one another. Then she kissed him. A long, lingering kiss. 'And it's your turn now because I've missed you too…'

CHAPTER NINE

'I HAVE A surprise for you,' Leandro's voice was low and lazy. He stroked her with one finger, trailing the feathery touch from her cheek along her shoulder blades and then dipping down to her cleavage.

Celia smiled and sighed, enjoying the familiar tingle his slightest touch produced in her.

They seemed to have spent the past five days in bed, a blissful orgy of love-making only interrupted by occasional sightseeing and food.

The sweeping swimming pool had largely remained unexplored and they had only actually gone to the beach once.

'Perhaps not the best of ideas…' Leandro had murmured, toying with her copper hair, twirling strands around his long, brown fingers, 'not with your colouring. You might burn.'

'There's a reason why sunblock was invented,' Celia had responded wryly, 'and, strangely, I tan pretty easily for a redhead. I must have inherited some of Dad's genes there.' But she had succumbed fast enough to the promise of what he had had in mind as an alternative.

She couldn't resist him. She would never be able to resist him. For now, she knew that it was mutual, but how long would that last for him? Surely not for ever, because the sweaty heat of passion always calmed and into that calm came the glory of contentment, but only if there was love as a stepping stone. Without that, there was always the danger that a replacement would be found to fill the vacuum.

Celia tried hard not to project into the future because their future was hardly straightforward with a baby in the mix. He was proving himself in so many ways he was probably not even aware of...proving himself in his kindness and his generosity, and she knew that that would translate into just the qualities that went into great parenting.

And the power of parenthood could be stronger than the tug of lust, especially for a man like Leandro, an honourable man who knew, from first-hand experience, the bitterness of an incomplete home. He was prepared to marry her for the sake of his baby and with that, he would surely realise, would come a curtailment of his freedoms? Once, she had wondered whether he might put their arrangement on a par with what he had had with Julie, but he and Julie had been platonic friends with the understanding written in from the start that they would discreetly take lovers, as need be.

That was quite different from what *they* shared. There would be no open doors when boredom with her kicked in, when he grew tired of the novelty of sleeping with her.

He would risk jeopardising the very thing he wanted to protect if he thought that he could look elsewhere, but would that be sufficient to stop him if and when that time arrived?

And what would she do if she were to be confronted with that situation?

These were uncomfortable questions that Celia thought it best to leave be. Why look for pain in advance? Why not throw herself into what they had and hope that the future was different from the one she predicted?

'A surprise?' she said now, still smiling, making sure her eyes didn't give away the tenderness she felt every time she looked at him. She had learned how to conceal what needed concealing and only revealed her emotions when he was asleep, when she could look at him with unguarded love.

'Last night here and then it's back to London.'

'I know.' She groaned and flung herself back to stare at the ceiling for a couple of seconds before facing him once again, stomach to stomach, their bodies pressed against one another. She grinned. 'I'd forgotten how nice it is being away from the grindstone for a bit.'

'We'll have a proper honeymoon later,' Leandro promised. 'Wherever you want to go.'

That was music to Celia's ears and she smiled. 'I'll start searching as soon as we're back,' she teased. 'Sure you can take more time off work?'

'I own it all. I can do whatever I want. If there's one thing money and power buy, it's freedom. That's all I ever wanted and I have it now, so yes. I can take whatever time I want away from the desk.'

'Were you and Julie planning on having a honeymoon?' Celia wasn't sure whether this question overstepped boundaries and then she decided that, as he was her husband-to-be, she should be free to overstep them. She would never ask him any question unless his answer couldn't hurt her. She would never ask him if he could ever love her…or how much she meant to him…those were lines her own self-defence mechanisms would never allow her to overstep, but everything else?

This was all part and parcel of the sort of *friendship* zone he had in mind, surely.

'No,' Leandro admitted without any hesitation. 'Ours was purely a business arrangement and, to be honest, Charles wouldn't have been too surprised at the lack of a honeymoon. He's always known me for the workaholic that I am. I expect, for the sake of appearances, we might have gone to some city or other for a weekend, but I would have worked and she would have shopped.'

'I guess *we* could have done that,' Celia mused. 'I mean, when you first thought about having one. It's not as though…well…'

'As though we were planning on picking up where we'd left off?' Leandro shifted, thinking that there was no way that *work* and *shopping* were going to be the only things they did. That would have been impossible.

'Tell me what the surprise is.'

'Dinner.'

'Dinner?'

'There won't be any air conditioning where we're going tonight and the views might be slightly different from what you've sampled before, but I'm hoping you enjoy the experience.' He grinned and began easing himself off the bed. 'We're being collected in an hour...so bath time, I think. Although...' his grin broadened and there was a glint of wicked invitation in his eyes '...we *could* have a bit more fun before we get changed...'

Celia took her time in the bath. Leandro was making calls. With the door to the bathroom open, she could dimly hear his deep voice and could picture him sprawled on the leather sofa in the sitting room, lazily telling his army of CEOs what to do and when.

She closed her eyes, wanting to relive everything they had done here since they'd come. She'd always led a sheltered life. Holidays were caravan parks and then, later, a rush of adrenaline when she'd gone on a ski holiday with her class to France. Then, in the blink of an eye, she and Martin were planning a future, heads in the clouds, and holidays were something not even on the agenda because they'd both been young and too broke to even buy a place to live.

She'd rushed headlong from that broken relationship to running her own business and trying to build it into something and, during those years, the very thought of a holiday was a joke.

So now? Overload. She'd managed to pack into a handful of days an entire lifetime's worth of gaping tourism.

They'd dined in a restaurant many floors up in their hotel and, sitting on beaded cushions, she had looked out through elegant arches to the stunning Burj Khalifa, which rose like a needle piercing the velvet sky. She'd been taken for a personal visit to a top falconer and seen how the birds were trained and watched as Leandro had handled one with unexpected expertise. She'd experienced the glitz and glamour of the Dubai Mall and been impressed by the architectural magnificence of the Burj Al Arab, a breathtaking testament to the bold contrasts that characterised the vibrant, bustling city. Everywhere was a fascinating mix of old and new, where the vibrancy of concrete, glass and stone nudged the stillness of the sand and sea.

Celia half guessed where they might be going but she was still impressed to death when they left the bright lights of the city behind and were driven out towards the open desert, an ocean of dark shapes and shadows, interrupted here and there with occasional bursts of bushes and trees.

Their driver played proud tour guide, told them about the history of Bedouin nomads who once called the land their home. All the while her eyes darted greedily out, shivering at the dark swirls and swells of sand while, next to her, Leandro's fingers curled into hers, setting alight all those forbidden emotions within her.

The utterly private Bedouin camp that greeted them took Celia's breath away. They were ushered into an enclosed area, which was incredible—with colourful rugs and lanterns and huge, hand-woven cushions and adorned with traditional relics.

'We could have spent the night here,' Leandro told her over the delicious hand-prepared meal that was brought in to them with a lot of pomp and ceremony, in various stages. 'There's a very nice and very small boutique hotel just a camel ride away. In fact, we'll go there before we head back so that we can freshen up and you can have a look at the pool. It's quite something. Fashioned to resemble an oasis. That said, I wanted to spend the last night here in our own bed with no one around...'

The lanterns flickered, creating a seductive, mellow atmosphere. The daytime heat had subsided and here, in the ornate tent, the air was fragrant with delicate incense and just the right side of warm. Celia had worn a floaty dress, perfectly buttoned up and respectful of all the dress codes of the country, but underneath the silk and cotton she felt the wetness pool between her legs and she pressed them together. Her mouth parted and Leandro fluttered his finger across her lips, touching her in a way that sent her pulses racing.

'We still have to finish the dessert course,' Celia breathed. 'And we can't leave without sampling the coffee. You know how proud they are of their coffee here...'

'Sadly you have a point, even though I'd like nothing more than to take that dress off you, button by button. Another time and another place...' He sat back with an elaborate sigh of resignation. 'We need to change the subject and urgently or else I'm going to have to make some kind of excuse and skip the dessert and coffee.'

Celia laughed. 'Okay. Tell me about Julie's dad and what's happening now that he's out of hospital... I had an email from Dan and apparently Julie's dad is over the moon at the upcoming wedding.'

'Yes.' Leandro grimaced. 'Julie and I decided that honesty was the best policy. We told him about the reason for the engagement. I'd half expected him to hit the roof, if I'm honest, but she knows her father better than

I do and she was right in guessing that, with his finances now in order and presented with a fait accompli, his pride wouldn't be a problem. He's also over the moon that his daughter has found true love, given the horror story of her first marriage.'

Celia looked down and squashed a sudden sharp pang of envy. She'd smiled at many a radiant bride-to-be, twisting and turning and beaming at a fitting, waxing lyrical about The Big Day, but this was the first time she'd ever felt envious at someone else's dream wedding. She knew why. This was the first time she was in the position of knowing that her own dream would never come true even though, cruelly, she was just so close. The baby…the wedding plans…the man of her dreams… *Just so happened that she wasn't the woman of his…*

For the rest of the night, while they finished their lavish meal, they skimmed the surface, chatting about all sorts of things. When Celia thought back to the arrogant guy who had shown up at her shop, setting her teeth on edge, she almost couldn't believe that they were here now.

Was he equally aware of how far they'd come?

There was a familiarity between them that

said so much. Did he recognise that as well? Or was he so embedded behind the walls he had built around himself that this was all just part and parcel of the friendship angle he felt they needed to cultivate? There was *lust* in one box and *friendship* in another box but there was no box for *love* because, for Leandro, that didn't exist.

Lust and friendship didn't add up, for him, the way they did for her to anything more than two separate emotions and the friendship element, she recognised, was only there at all because of the situation in which they found themselves.

For what they had to work, they had to get along. That was the practical approach and Leandro was practical and solution based.

If she had dug her heels in and refused to marry him because she wanted to be with someone who loved her, then she wondered if he might have been tempted to simply approach it from the solution-based angle that marriage would still be a good thing because a child needed two parents. So what was needed? A wife even if that wife wasn't the birth mother.

Celia didn't like thinking like that, but she knew that she had to protect herself somehow and being realistic was as good a protection as any. She wouldn't beat herself up if sometimes, in her quiet moments or when she was just lying in his arms, she hoped for more. She was only human, after all! She just wouldn't let *hoping for more* overtake *having her eyes wide open.*

'You've gone quiet.' This as they were back in the four-wheel drive and bumping away from the mysterious shape-shifting dunes, back to the bright twinkling lights of the city.

'Have I?' Celia plastered a bright smile on her face but it felt a little strained.

'Tired?'

'And very, very full.'

'Not too tired and full, I hope…?'

Sex was uppermost on his mind, she thought, and, while it thrilled her, for once she would have liked to have told him how she was really feeling and the doubts that were crawling through her like bothersome insects that wouldn't go away.

She pictured his face closing up and the shutters being pulled down. They had an arrangement and, without anything in writing, the terms and conditions of their arrangement were clear.

'It's being pregnant.' She yawned, veering away from the powerful tug of honesty. 'Something to do with the hormones, I guess.'

'Celia, my apologies. It never occurred to me...'

Celia heard the genuine concern in his voice and relaxed. He might never love her, but he would love their child, of that she was one hundred per cent sure.

'It's okay.' She laughed, relaxing. 'I'm pretty new to this as well. I only recognise the symptoms as and when they occur!'

'Okay...so tiredness and easily full...'

'Leandro, the meal was enormous.'

'What other signs and symptoms should I be on the lookout for?'

'I think pregnant women can sometimes get a little over-emotional.' Celia laid some groundwork just in case she needed it to come to her rescue in the future.

'I don't think that's confined to pregnant women,' Leandro drawled. 'Perhaps I should download a book...'

'You would download a book on pregnancy just to find out what you should look out for?'

'Amongst other things...'

'I thought you only read work-related tomes and heavy-duty biographies for light relief?' she teased.

'You make me sound like a bundle of laughs.' He looked at her with an easy grin.

The bright lights of the hotel were ahead

of them and suddenly she really did feel tired even though she'd been buzzing all night.

'It's nice that you want to actually read a pregnancy manual. I can't think that many guys would be interested in doing that.'

'Like I keep telling you, I'm not like many guys and, besides, that's what we're all about, isn't it?'

Celia stilled and then was glad for the distraction of the car stopping and the doors being opened by the uniformed porters outside and then hurrying inside the hotel, out of the sticky night-time heat.

'I mean,' Leandro picked up when she'd hoped he might just have left it off, 'this isn't about us, this is about the baby we've made together, so it's only right that I find out as much as I can about the business of pregnancy and giving birth and what I will be required to do. It's new to you and it's new to me as well.'

For once, she wasn't desperate to get her clothes off when they entered their suite of rooms and, strangely, he seemed equally reticent.

She felt sticky and ever so slightly depressed and when she excused herself to go have a bath, he nodded without demur.

'Get you something cold to drink?' he offered, once again the very essence of kind consideration and reminding her, without even having to try, that this was first and foremost what he was about. Her welfare was his concern because she was carrying his baby. 'The apricot juice is excellent. You might find it refreshing. It's been a long evening, perhaps too long given your condition.'

Celia smiled tightly. Irritation surged through her. She knew she was being unfair, but she was still smarting from his casual reminder that what they had was all about the baby yet to be born. None of it was about *her*. He fancied her for the moment but essentially *she* didn't matter.

And the fact that he was now treating her like a piece of porcelain made her even more irritated.

Was this how she would be treated as time wore on and the sex dimmed?

'Apricot juice would be…lovely…'

'Sure you're okay?'

Celia bit back a sarcastic retort that would get neither of them anywhere and might even start erecting the sort of invisible barriers she would later find difficult to dismantle.

'If this doesn't work out between us, Leandro…what happens next?'

'Whoa. Where did *that* come from?' His

brows knitted and his dark eyes were a little cooler now, a little more watchful and bemused.

Celia shrugged and looked away.

'I thought we had a good time tonight,' he said slowly.

'We did.'

'I *thought* we were doing a damn good job of getting to know one another.'

'We are.'

'Then where are you now heading with this?'

'Nowhere.' Celia looked at him, held his gaze, her eyes steady and as unreadable as his were.

'I'm thinking,' Leandro murmured, 'that *nowhere* isn't a direction for the questions you're asking.'

'I'm just tired, that's all.' She felt panicked at the box she'd opened because she knew that certain boxes, given their situation, were best left shut.

'There's only so far you can run with that excuse, Celia. That's not the first time this evening you've told me that you're tired and it's beginning to sound like a sticking plaster being put onto something that's really bugging you.' He led the way to the sofa and beckoned her across.

He patted next to him and when she sat

down he immediately turned to her, his eyes penetrating and intense, searching her face to get inside her head and find out what was going on.

'So? Are you going to spit it out or are we going to go round the houses playing guessing games?'

'I suppose we've discussed a lot of things,' Celia muttered, one foot hovering over the edge of a cliff she'd been so determined not to go anywhere near. 'We've talked about the practicalities like where we're going to live and what the choices are for me after the baby's born. We've discussed whether we would get a nanny if I decide to return to work and *when* returning to work might be appropriate…'

'But…? Because I can hear the siren sound of a *but*.'

'*And* I think that this has been a fantastic few days getting to know one another…'

'Agreed.' Leandro smiled with wolfish sexiness that made Celia's bones feel like mush.

'But lust and sex don't last for ever…'

Leandro frowned. 'We have yet to put that to the test.'

'Maybe we should try and work out what we might do if and when that time comes.'

'Why?'

'What do you mean *why*?'

'Why pre-empt a situation that's nowhere on the horizon?'

'Because…'

'There are no guarantees in life, Celia.' His eyes were serious and he was leaning into her, which had the effect of jumbling her thoughts until she wasn't sure quite what she'd been trying to say in the first place. Her hands itched to touch him and to smooth over the crease that had suddenly appeared between them, like a ripple disturbing the flat, smooth surface of a lake.

'I get that.'

'We do our best and if problems arise at a later date, then that's the time to try and sort them out.'

'Yes, well…'

'You want to turn this into a list of pros and cons and I don't think that's a good idea. We both know what we have to do, what the right thing to do is…don't we?' He inclined his head to one side and gave her a few seconds to respond, which she did by nodding. Not vigorously but sufficiently for him to nod firmly in return, in agreement with her. 'We've talked at length about this,' he said quietly. 'In the end, there's nothing in life that's one hundred per cent guaranteed. Nothing. The rate of divorce says it all, wouldn't you agree? People walk down the aisle with big dreams and big hopes but two thirds of those starry-eyed couples will see the inside of a divorce court sooner or later. What we have will be sturdier, trust me.'

Celia was the first to look away.

'You're right.' But she had to try and inject conviction into her voice and remind herself of all the reasons why what they had was better than the alternative. She might be greedy for more, but greed was no reason to start unpicking what had been knitted together. When she smiled, there was more warmth and she stood up and told him that she was going to have a bath.

'I have so many baths and showers here.' She did her best to get things back on track.

'It's the heat.' Leandro followed suit and stood up, towering over her, his dark eyes still concerned and still ever so slightly watchful. 'Relax. I'll hunt down some juice for you from the cafe downstairs. It's open twenty-four-seven and I could do with stretching my legs.'

Celia kept smiling even though there was a wariness in his voice that dismayed her. Instead of relaxing in the bath, she opted for a quick shower and then, on the spur of the moment and instead of climbing into bed, she changed into a pair of loose dark culottes and a grey silk top and headed down to the cafe.

She knew where he had gone because it was the cafe that was transformed into the breakfast area in the morning.

There were several five-star restaurants in the complex and the cafe was the least formal of all.

At a little after eleven, it was still busy, with people coming and going. The crowd were all elegant, expensively dressed, and the mix of different languages as they chattered past her made Celia smile. This was a land of such contrasts, a place where people converged from all over the world, rich in diversity and ancient in its heritage.

Which made her think of the perfect evening they had shared at the desert. Leandro had put real thought into doing something special on their last evening in Dubai and he would have been utterly perplexed by the way she had thrown the gesture back in his face.

This wasn't about *him*. This was about *her* and it suddenly felt imperative that she set things back on the right track.

Fired up with a new sense of purpose, Celia almost missed Leandro because she was so certain that she would find him at the long mirrored bar, which was still buzzing with people.

Standing in the doorway, she looked around, taking in the huge room as a whole. It was cleverly divided by tall, leafy trees in huge urns, and circular seating wrapped around marble-topped tables sectioned off private seating areas. Elsewhere, there were low, informal sofas with tables and more formal arrangements for dining.

Mostly people were standing with just a handful of diners sitting at some of the tables, having heaven only knew what manner of late-night snacks.

Eyes flitting then returning to the tall, languid figure leaning against the wall at the back, Celia felt her heart begin to beat fast.

Leandro was holding the glass of apricot juice and he was chatting to a young woman so stunningly beautiful that she took Celia's breath away.

Her hair was short and sharp and raven-black and she was slender as a willow, wearing figure-hugging trousers and a bright red top that managed to be prim and ridiculously sexy at the same time.

She saw Leandro glance at his watch, smile, prepare to move off.

Nothing about his demeanour spoke of

anything suspicious at all. He wasn't standing too close to his companion and his expression was polite and friendly, but nothing more than that.

So why did she suddenly feel as though the world were tilting on its axis?

Old insecurities rose up with a vengeance and she was catapulted unfairly back to how she had felt when she had found out that Martin had found someone else, someone tall and beautiful and quite the opposite of *her*.

She'd felt *wanting*. It was the same feeling that hit her now like a wave and she stood there, eyes wide, trembling and trying to kill the feeling because there was no place for it in this scenario.

But she was rooted to the spot.

Leandro, on the other side of the room, was startled because he'd been chatting to the Princess for longer than he'd thought but out of politeness it had been impossible for him to get away.

She'd spotted him and hived off from the group of friends she had come with so that she could tell him all about the latest family sagas, of which there were many.

Leandro had met Leila several times and had helped her with various university application forms, guiding her in her choice of subject and giving her the rundown on what Cambridge as a town was like because that had been her choice of university.

But even as he'd been chatting, his mind had been taken up with Celia.

He'd hated her withdrawal. It had made him realise how much he'd become accustomed to the easiness that existed between them. The silences between them were as comfortable as the chat and for Leandro that said a lot, although he was only now realising how much.

He glanced idly at the exit, ready to make his polite excuses because a tipsy Princess looked set to talk for England while her bodyguards, discreetly positioned by the bar, tried to stifle their yawns.

He saw Celia just as she spotted him and their eyes met, homing in on each other and eliminating everything else that was extraneous, from the milling late-night crowd to the sound of talk and laughter. The expression on her face was open and honest before she had time to think about adjusting it.

She was...*hurt.*

'Excuse me, Leila, I really have to go—'

'So soon, Leandro? Come join us for dinner!'

Leandro smiled but he was already straightening and his eyes were still on Celia. 'I feel my age enough as it is chatting to you, Leila. Ten minutes surrounded by your peers and the hair on my head will start going grey!'

He detached himself, headed towards the exit to where Celia hadn't moved although her expression had smoothed over, was now polite and distant.

'What are you doing here?' he asked. He ushered her away from the cafe, back into the lobby and towards the bank of lifts, still holding the juice in one hand.

He didn't do *hurt* from women when it came to his personal life. He never had. He had never welcomed the sensation of being penned in or the irritating feeling that he should be justifying himself in any way. As far as Leandro was concerned, there was a thin line between questioning his motives and nagging him into toeing a line he had never had any intention of toeing.

The claustrophobia of Celia's jealousy, because jealousy was surely what he had glimpsed, fleeting but all too apparent, was not welcome.

He didn't expect or court jealousy in women. He didn't like it because…of what it said. Celia was jealous because she cared. The thought of that was ice in his veins. With the force of muscle memory ingrained for more years than he cared to remember, Leandro's aversion to the swirl of that forbidden emotion rammed into him with the force of a sledgehammer. He wasn't built to return emotion, to return love. It just wasn't in his DNA and the need to repel was as instinctive as drawing breath.

She was walking alongside him, head held high, explaining that having a shower had woken her up and she'd decided to come down and perhaps have her drink in the cafe rather than wait for him to bring it up to her. Her voice was light enough as she repeated the mantra about not wanting to be treated like a china doll just because she was expecting.

But she wasn't looking at him and he wanted her to.

'I expect,' he cut through the chatter just as the lift doors opened to their floor, 'that you're going to ask me who I was talking to…' He could feel himself shutting down inside, sealing himself off because that was just what he was programmed to do. What was wrong with that? What was wrong with self-protection? He'd built his life around it.

Celia looked at him for the first time since he had joined her where she'd been frozen to the spot in the cafe. She had to school her

features into a mask of smooth, casual indif-
ference. She was hurting inside so much that
it felt as though a knife were twisting inside
her, but this was what she had signed up to
and she would find a way of dealing with it.

'No,' she said tonelessly. 'I wasn't. You're
not a prisoner, Leandro, and, as you've said
too many times to count, this is a marriage of
convenience. We both know why we're doing
what we're doing but I suppose it does bring
me back to what I was trying to say to you
earlier...'

'Which is what?'

'What happens when the lust dies? Do you
start looking elsewhere?' She paused and
then said, sotto voce, 'Or do I? We never quite
addressed that, Leandro, and yes, it might be
good to live in the moment and cross bridges
when we get to them but maybe we're being
naïve. Maybe we need to deal with what
happens...'

CHAPTER TEN

LEANDRO DIDN'T SAY ANYTHING. He nudged open the heavy door to the suite. He could feel a cold thread of something... *What was that emotion? Surely it wasn't fear?* It rippled through him and in that very instant he realised that the terms of the contract had changed.

How had that happened?

He was always the one in control, always the one who called the shots and yet now, as he looked at the cool, determined expression on her face, he knew that the role had been reversed.

Old instincts died hard, though. A primal revulsion at the thought of anyone else having a say over him, over his thoughts and decision, roared into life, obliterating everything else in its path.

'Maybe we do.' He held her gaze for a couple of seconds, then strode off towards the kitchen where he dumped the now forgotten glass of apricot juice so that he could help himself to a glass of cold water. Frankly, he could have done with something stronger.

He felt rather than saw her pace to the kitchen behind him and his pulses quickened.

'You were hurt.' Leandro dumped the empty glass on the pale, glossy counter and folded his arms.

'Yes,' Celia said quietly. 'I was hurt even though I knew that I had no right to be.'

'Why?' Leandro demanded.

'Because I foolishly trusted you...' Celia's heart was beating fast. He had seen her, had seen the expression on her face before she had had time to conceal it and he was astute enough when it came to reading women to know what had been going through her head. All the pitfalls to this arrangement were suddenly laid bare and, while she would much rather have not had to face up to them just yet, maybe it was all for the best that they did. Marriage was a solid commitment and not to be taken lightly. She'd dithered and agonised over what would happen without Love as the glue to bind them, not as parents but as two human beings sharing a life together.

She'd pretended a lot of things to herself from the very first moment she had slept with Leandro. Before even.

She'd pretended that she wasn't attracted to him, and then when she'd faced that one down and accepted the truth, she'd kidded herself that fancying someone was a far cry from having feelings for them.

What a joke!

How could she ever have swept every core value she'd grown up with under the carpet?

And yet that was what she had done. She'd managed to convince herself that she could be like him, that she could detach, and of course she couldn't.

What a mess. How on earth could she have contemplated a life in love with a guy who wasn't in love with her? This very moment was always going to come, the moment when she knew that he would always be attracted to other women. He might not consider doing anything with any of them, not now at any rate, but how long would that situation last?

The very fact that he had no desire to at least defend himself against what he knew she would have been thinking pretty much said it all.

'And what have I done that makes you as-

sume you can't trust me? I've been honest
with you from day one, honest about...the
man I am...'

'So you have. I don't want to have this conversation standing up here.' She spun round
on her heel and padded towards the sitting
room to perch, arms clasped tightly around
herself. She looked at him as he sat on the
chair opposite her but then he pulled it closer
and leaned forwards so that he was crowd-
ing her.

'I thought I could do this,' Celia said quietly. 'Even when I saw you there, talking to
that woman—'

'Friend,' Leandro interrupted, 'talking to
that *friend*. I know Leila's father. I've met
her a few times in the past and she's like a
sister to me.'

Celia blushed but she wasn't going to apologise for jumping to the wrong conclusion
because it didn't make any difference.

'Whatever...'

'No!' Leandro all but roared. 'It's not a case
of *whatever*!' He vaulted upright, raked his
fingers through his hair but just as quickly
sat back down, his body language urgent and
demanding.

It was late but he hardly noticed the hour.
No deal, however big, no decision, however

life-changing, had ever occupied his attention the way it was occupied now.

'It would have happened sooner or later,' Celia told him gently. 'I know we both had the best of intentions going into this and I wish so much that I could carry on believing that those good intentions would be enough to see us through but, for me, they just won't be.'

'Don't say that. You've barely given this a chance.'

'It's…it's not got anything to do with giving it a chance.'

'We get along, Celia. You know we do. And we're one hundred per cent compatible in bed—'

'I was hurt,' she interrupted him bluntly, 'when I saw you with that girl. I suppose I knew in my heart that there was nothing going on there—'

'Then what is all this about?'

'If you'd just let me finish, Leandro…' She breathed in deeply, but it was difficult to meet his piercing gaze. 'I wasn't just hurt when I saw you with…that woman. I was *jealous*.'

Celia's heart sank as she saw him get exactly where she was going with this. Hurt was a very different animal from jealousy.

'And just then, at that very moment,' she continued quietly, 'I realised how impossible life was going to be with you, not despite the fact that we get along and we're compatible in bed. Impossible *because* we get along and we're compatible in bed. If I could treat this like you, as a business transaction, then it would be fine.'

'You make it sound as though it's deprived of all emotion.'

'It's deprived of one essential emotion. At least it is for me.'

'I don't do love.'

'I get that, which is why I'm calling the whole thing off.'

'This is crazy,' Leandro grated, ashen.

'Mum and Dad are going to be disappointed but it's better for them to be disappointed than for me to face heartbreak every single day because I don't want to face disappointing them.' She paused and then continued, in the same low, even voice, 'And before you tell me that it's always better for a child to have both parents, I would say that you're right but only if both parents are happy. You might be happy but I wouldn't be, not really.'

'You have my word that I would never be unfaithful.'

Celia didn't say anything for a bit because she knew that this would be a big thing for Leandro.

What was he promising her? Were there things being said between the lines?

Hope sprang eternal. Celia knew that. She also knew that, for her own sanity, it wasn't something she should cling to. Besides, what was said now could easily be forgotten in times to come. Leandro was a man accustomed to getting what he wanted at whatever cost. It would not probably even occur to him that he might be toying with the truth when he made a promise like that.

'I'm going to hit the sack now.' She stood up, just about managing to avoid bumping into him. She was already missing him! All her clothes were in the bedroom they had been sharing but tonight she would be sleeping in one of the other two rooms.

She grabbed her clothes quickly, half expecting him to follow but he didn't. When she left the room they had shared, he was standing in the sitting room and as ill at ease as she had ever seen him.

'I'm going to head down to the bar. I need a drink.' He shoved his hands in his pockets and stared at her, but Celia shrugged and mumbled something along the lines of *okay*.

'What time will we be leaving in the morning?'

'We will leave the hotel around eleven.' His mouth twisted into a parody of a mocking smile. 'That gives us some uncomfortable time to spend in one another's company. Do you think you'll be able to do that or are we to abandon our attempts at friendship on the back of everything you've just said?'

'No!' Celia took a couple of steps towards him. She felt the prick of tears stinging the backs of her eyes. 'This isn't what I wanted,' she cried, stricken. 'It's important that we maintain a good relationship...'

'I feel,' Leandro said heavily, 'that we took two steps forward and then, suddenly, fifteen back.'

'Because I broke the rules and decided to be honest with you?'

'Because you changed the rules halfway through, without warning.'

'I'll see you in the morning, Leandro.' They weren't going to get anywhere, going over the same old ground. Celia turned away, aware of his eyes on her, and she only sagged with relief when the bedroom door was closed, then she leant against it, drawing in ragged breaths.

How had it all come to this? How had she gone from *A bit of Leandro is better than none at all* to *I just can't go through with this*?

Seeing him with another woman. That was how. That was what had brought home to her just how tough it would be to face an uncertain future, always wondering when he might stray, always aching somewhere deep, deep inside, prematurely grieving something that would happen at some point in the future.

Yes, it would be horrible having a lifelong connection with him and watching him move on with his life, but at least she might be able to move on with hers. At least he wouldn't be there, living under the same roof, with a wedding ring on her finger reminding her that this was her life and there was nothing she could do to change it.

Celia fell into fitful sleep, having changed into a baggy tee shirt and the soft shorts she had brought over to sleep in, before sleeping naked had become the order of the day. She wished she'd brought all her clothes across. She should have done that when he'd disappeared for a drink. If she'd done that, she would have been able to kill some time packing to leave in the morning. As it was, she nodded off to the bright light on her phone updating her on what was happening in the news back in the UK.

She wasn't aware, two hours later, of the soft knock on her bedroom door.

On the other side of that door, Leandro waited, torn between knocking again or bailing.

He'd gone for a drink but had ended up on strong coffee instead.

Everything had been going along swimmingly so Celia's revelations had come as a body blow. Of course, he had accepted that life as he knew it had been irrevocably changed the second she had told him about the pregnancy. If he had been a little surprised at how easily he had assimilated that change into his psyche, then he had simply put it down to his expertise at dealing with what life threw at him.

He had been more astonished at how passionately he had felt about the baby she was carrying.

He'd gone from the prospect of fatherhood not being anywhere remotely on his radar to it being the most important thing in his life. Why else would he have agreed with alacrity to sacrifice his way of life? Without question?

But there *had* been clauses, he'd thought, as he'd stared down into his cup of black coffee an hour previously.

He'd brought the same clauses to marriage as he had brought to their fling when they'd been trapped by snow in Scotland. *No love... no emotional anchor being sunk to the bottom of the ocean...*

He'd expected her to fall in line and do the

right thing because *he* was prepared to do so. And she had. She'd agreed because she was someone rooted in doing what was morally right. He hadn't had to beg because she was unselfish by nature and traditional enough to acquiesce to the overriding importance of family. She wasn't someone who was trained to put herself first.

Leandro had realised, as the thoughts had piled up in his head, that he had been lazy.

He'd read so much of her and enjoyed it all but he hadn't bothered to join the dots to see the road ahead.

He'd grown accustomed to her openness, her refreshing honesty and that way she had of looking at him that made him feel a hundred metres tall.

He'd sunk himself into their love-making and become addicted to it.

In every single way, he had luxuriated in her giving and her affection and her warm, supportive, empathetic conversation that had seen him open up in ways he never had before, and still he had kept reminding her of the boundaries to what they had. He'd stuck to what he knew without bothering to analyse why. It was who he was and what he did and he hadn't questioned it.

And he'd watched her fall in love with him without considering the ramifications.

Worse, he'd watched *himself* falling in love with her and completely ignored the signs because falling in love had never been in his remit.

Which brought him here now, with his hand raised to knock on the door again.

Except was it going to be too little too late? He would bare his soul, but would it seem too coincidental? Would she think that he was simply playing a card from his hand in the hope of bringing her back on board? Manufacturing his words into what she wanted him to say?

He knocked on the door, this time a little more forcefully, and then he gently pushed it open to stand, framed in the doorway, for a couple of seconds.

Celia had dimly been aware of *a sound* but it was only when Leandro knocked for a second time that she blinked and rubbed her eyes and realised that someone was at the bedroom door and, since there were only two of them in this presidential suite, there was no mystery as to who her caller was.

She sat up, on full alert, and stared at Leandro backlit in the doorway.

Was he drunk? Had he come on the back of several whiskies to try and make her change her mind? She tightened her lips. She wasn't going to start arguing because he was right, they needed to keep their lines of communication open. But she wasn't going to cave in either.

'I'm sorry.'

Those two words were enough to give her a jolt.

'What are you doing here?'

She had left the light voile curtains pulled and the shutters open and, through the slats, moonlight illuminated the bedroom. He didn't sound drunk.

'I…can I come in? I won't sit on the bed. Don't worry. I can…pull a chair…please.'

Please. Another word to undermine her defences.

'You can't change my mind, Leandro.'

'I… I'm not here to do that. I'm here because I find I have no choice.'

'You're talking in riddles.'

'Let me come in. Please, Celia. If you don't want me to, then that's fine. I will stand right here and say what I have to say.'

'Have you been drinking?'

'Black coffee.' He half smiled. 'I'd aimed for stronger but realised that, when it came to getting my thoughts in order, whisky on the rocks wasn't going to work in my favour.'

The *please* along with the *I'm sorry* had got to her, and, with a click of impatience with her own weakness, she nodded curtly and told him that he could come in but that she was tired and that he shouldn't think for a second that she was going to have a change of mind.

'I do want to change your mind,' Leandro said in a low voice. 'More than anything else I want to change your mind but, even more than that, I want you to be happy and if being happy means letting you go, then I'll do that.'

'You will? Is this…some sort of game you're playing, Leandro?'

'I've never been more serious in my life before. I was sleepwalking, Celia, and it took you telling me how you feel about me to wake me up.'

'I don't need reminding of that,' Celia said stiffly.

'It took guts.' Leandro met her eyes. 'More guts than I've had.'

'Don't say things you don't mean,' Celia whispered. As fast as she tried to squash it, hope flared, a little flame that refused to be extinguished. She hated it yet couldn't stop it.

'I'm saying things… I never thought I'd

ever say but you told me you loved me and suddenly everything fell into place. I've spent my life accepting that love and everything that went along with it wasn't for me. It was no great loss. I saw my father's life and I worked out before I even hit my teens that what he had wasn't what I wanted. I heard him crying at night and putting his dreams in a box and throwing away the key because my mother left him. Well, you know all this because I've said as much. Truth is, the very fact that I said that much to you should have set alarm bells ringing in my head.'

'What do you mean?' Unconsciously, Celia was straining towards him. Caution warred with simmering excitement because every word that left his mouth rang with heartfelt sincerity. She weakly tried to remember the dangers of believing what you wanted to believe.

'I made my mind up about a lot of things,' Leandro said quietly, 'when I was too young to know that life isn't something you can plan out like a military campaign. I forgot about nuance. Then you came along and that's what you brought to my life. I didn't want it and I didn't like it, but I was powerless to resist it.' He sighed. 'So, I guess, what I've come to say is this: I'm in love with you.' He held up both his hands in a gesture of weary resignation. 'I know what you're going to say and I can't blame you, Celia. You're going to tell me that you don't believe a word I'm saying and I shall have to accept that.'

'You would do that?'

'I want you to marry me, Celia, for real. For love. I need you to believe me when I say that, but…if I've left it too late then, yes, I will never bother you again, but I will never be the man you made me again. So will you marry me? Be my wife? Grow old with me and have a dozen more kids with me?'

Celia flung all doubt out of the window and threw herself at him, at this wonderful guy she loved with all her might.

'Yes, yes, yes, yes!' She laughed and half sobbed and covered him with kisses. 'Except for the dozen kids…although…' she smiled and this time kissed him tenderly '…who knows what the future holds?'

The wedding, three months later, couldn't have been more perfect.

That first dress would never have an outing, destined to remained preserved behind plastic for ever, a reminder of what, thankfully, had never been.

But the simple ivory dress she created for herself, with the help of her two enthusiastic assistants, was perfect in every detail, from the white soft folds like petals along the hem, that reminded her of the falling snow in Scotland, to the pink delicately woven beads and rosebuds that made her think of the glorious sunrises in Dubai. She got her opportunity to walk up the aisle of the little church her parents attended and all her friends and relatives, past and present, were there for the ceremony.

And if she was showing her baby bump? Leandro couldn't have been more proud. He couldn't take his eyes off her. The honeymoon, which was now planned post baby and when all the settling into their new house was done and dusted, would be to the Maldives.

'Sun,' he had promised two months previously, 'sand, sea and sex. Don't forget the dozen babies you promised me...'

'Let's just get baby number one out of the way first.' She had laughed.

And baby number one was born three days early and arrived with no fuss, although Leandro had been prepared for all and every eventuality.

He had downloaded the latest baby book and

had passed many a contented evening squirming at some of the more graphic details.

Yet, when the time came for her to go to the hospital, he was more nervous than she was.

Tomasina Elizabeth Diaz.

His father, Tomas, had been over the moon and so had Celia's mother, Lizzie.

But Lizzie Drew had more than her cupful of joy, for Dan and Julie, whose wedding had been low-key on a beach in Scotland followed by a reception at Leandro's country estate there, were also expecting their first child.

All those strands that had seemed to float in disarray had been woven together.

'Penny for them.'

Strands…accidental meetings and quirks of fate… *Those* were the things that had been occupying Celia's mind as she'd gazed at her six-week-old daughter, who was fast asleep in her Moses basket, oblivious to her parents sitting on the sofa next to the basket, lazily watching telly and sporadically chatting.

What better way to spend an evening, one of their first, in the sweetest cottage they had found in a little village in Berkshire?

'Do you ever think what might have happened…?'

'If your brother hadn't been in the right

place at the right time delivering a book to you? If he had never crossed paths with Julie?'

Leandro pulled her to him and engulfed her in his arms before tilting her chin so that their eyes met, his openly loving and deadly serious.

'I try not to think about that,' he told her truthfully, 'but yes. Who can ignore the co-incidences that have led us to this place, right here and right now? I'm the happiest man on earth because of you but you're right...if Dan hadn't met Julie...if snow hadn't stopped them from reaching my place in Scotland, hadn't locked us into a bubble and made lovers out of us...if an accidental pregnancy hadn't brought you back into my life.' He paused then added, thoughtfully, 'No... I would still have come back to you, my darling, whether you had returned to my life or not. It might have taken a bit longer because I was a stubborn fool too set in his ways for his own good, but I would have come right back to you because *not* coming back to you would have been unthinkable.'

'Right answer,' Celia said with a sigh of pure contentment.

'Now...while our precious Tomasina gives us a moment of free time, shall we...?'

Leandro stood, pulling Celia up with him and then holding her tight to kiss her long and slow on the lips.

'I can't think of anything better,' Celia gurgled, smiling and hugging him as they headed for the bedroom.

* * * * *

If you were blown away by
Bound by a Nine-Month Confession
why not dive into these other
Cathy Williams stories?

Promoted to the Italian's Fiancée
Claiming His Cinderella Secretary
Desert King's Surprise Love-Child
Consequences of Their Wedding Charade
Hired by the Forbidden Italian

Available now!